D0411328

THE
Game

Other titles by Diana Wynne Jones

Chrestomanci Series
Charmed Life*
The Magicians of Caprona*
Witch Week*
The Lives of Christopher Chant*
Mixed Magics*
Conrad's Fate*
The Pinhoe Egg

Archer's Goon*
Black Maria*
Castle in the Air*
Dogsbody
Eight Days of Luke
The Homeward Bounders
Howl's Moving Castle*
The Merlin Conspiracy*
The Ogre Downstairs
Power of Three
Stopping for a Spell
A Tale of Time City
Wilkins' Tooth

For older readers
Fire and Hemlock
Hexwood
The Time of the Ghost

For younger readers
Wild Robert

*Also available on audio

HarperCollins *Children's Books*

First published in the USA by Firebird,
an imprint of Penguin Group (USA) Inc 2007
First published in Great Britain by
HarperCollins Children's Books 2008
Harper Collins Children's Books is a
division of HarperCollins Publishers Ltd
77-85 Fulham Palace Road,
Hammersmith, London, W6 8JB

www.harpercollinschildrensbooks.co.uk
www.dianawynnejones.com

1 3 5 7 9 8 6 4 2

ISBN 13: 978 0 00 726379 0
ISBN 10: 0 00 726379 1

Printed and bound in Great Britain by
Clays Ltd, St Ives plc

This one is for Frances

Chapter One

When Hayley arrived at the big house in Ireland, bewildered and in disgrace, rain was falling and it was nearly dark. Her cousin Mercer had called the place just "the Castle". As far as Hayley could see, peering up at the place while Cousin Mercer was paying the taxi, the building was a confusing mixture of house and castle and barn. She could see turrets and sharply sloping roofs, tall chimneys, a wooden wall and a stone part at one side that seemed to have been patched up with new bricks. Then the taxi drove off in a spurt of mud.

Cousin Mercer – who had confused Hayley all along by turning out to be a grown up youngish man and not a cousin her own age – picked up Hayley's small old-fashioned suitcase and hurried her into the house, where it was more than ever confusing.

They came into a large stone-floored dining room full of people milling about around the enormous dining table, or in and out of the big kitchen beyond. Most of them were children, but all older-seeming and larger than Hayley, while distracted-looking ladies, who were probably aunts, pushed this way and that among them with piles of plates and baskets of bread.

Nobody took any notice of Hayley at all. True, somebody said, "Good. She's here. Now we can eat at last", but nobody really looked at her. Cousin Mercer left Hayley standing beside her suitcase and threaded his way to the kitchen, shouting, "Mother! Sorry about this. The plane was late and the taxi driver lost the way!"

Hayley stood. Her arms hung slightly outwards from the rest of her and her hands dangled, useless and floppy with strangeness. She had never been in the same room with so many people in her life. She was used to the hushed and sequestered way Grandma and Grandad lived, where nobody ran about or laughed much, and nobody *ever* shouted. These people were so lively and so *loud*. She didn't know who any of them were, apart from Cousin Mercer who had brought her here from England, and she missed her friend Flute acutely, even though it was probably Flute's fault that she was here and in disgrace. She still didn't understand how she had made Grandma so angry.

Hayley sighed. The other main thing about these tall, rushing, shouting children was that they all wore jeans or long baggy trousers with lots of pockets down the sides, and bright stripy tops. Hayley sadly realised that her neat floral dress and her shiny patent-leather shoes were quite wrong for this place. She wished she had jeans and trainers too, but Grandma disapproved of trousers for girls.

To add to the strangeness, there were more boys here than girls. Most of the boys were fair and skinny, like the girls – and the girls were so pretty and so confident that Hayley sighed again – but two of the boys stood out by being dark. One was a tall, calm boy who didn't seem to shout as much as the others. He was obviously popular, because the others were always trying to get his attention. "*Troy!*" they shouted. "Come and look at my new trick!" or "Troy! What do you think of *this*?" Troy always grinned and went obligingly over to look.

The other dark boy was smaller and he struck Hayley as a perfect little beast. He spent his time slyly pulling the beautiful streaming hair of the girls, or stamping on people's feet, or trying to steal things out of the pockets in the baggy trousers. Hayley learnt his name too, because every minute or so someone screamed, "Tollie, do that again and you'll *die*!"

These people are all my cousins! Hayley thought wonderingly. And I didn't know about any of them until this moment!

Here she found that Tollie had come to stand in front of her, jeeringly, with his hands hanging in exactly the same useless position that Hayley's were and his feet planted the same uncertain six inches apart. "Yuk!" he said. "You dirty outcast!"

"You're my cousin," Hayley said. Her voice came out small and prim with nerves.

"Nim-pim!" Tollie mimicked her. "I am *not* so your cousin! Mercer's my dad and *he's* your cousin. But you're only a dirty outcast in a frilly dress."

Hayley felt things boiling in her that she would rather not know. She wanted to leap on Tollie and pull pieces off him – ears, nose, fingers, hair, she scarcely cared which, so long as they came away with lots of *blood* – but luckily at that moment a large lady bustled up and enfolded Hayley against her big soft bosom hung with many hard strings of beads.

"My dear!" the lady said. "Forgive me. I was making the sauce and you know how it goes all lumpy if you leave it. I'm your Aunt May. Tollie, go away and stop being a pain. You have to forgive Tollie, my dear. Most of the year he's the only child here, but this is the week we have all the family to stay and he feels outnumbered. Now come and be introduced to everyone."

Hayley, who had gone limp with relief against Aunt May's many necklaces, found herself tensing up again at this. Now they were *all* going to despise her.

Although nobody did seem to despise her, the introductions left Hayley almost as confused as before.

The loud, fair cousins were the children of two different aunts. But, beyond gathering that some were Laxtons and belonged to Aunt Geta, and that the rest were Tighs, which made them sons and daughters of Aunt Celia, Hayley had no idea which were which – let alone what all their names were.

Aunt Geta stood out a bit by being tall and fair, with an impeccable neatness about her, like a picture painted very strictly inside the lines. Grandma would approve of Aunt Geta, Hayley thought. But Aunt Celia was a blurred sort of person. Aunt Alice, who didn't seem to have any children, was like a film star, almost unreal she was so perfect. And the tall, calm Troy turned out to be the son of another aunt who had stayed at home in Scotland. Most confusingly of all, the slender brown lady, whose little pearl earrings echoed the curves of her long cheeks and the shine of her big dark eyes, turned out not to be an aunt at all, but Troy's elder sister, Harmony. Since Harmony had been bustling about just like the aunts, setting the table and telling Tollie and the Tighs and Laxtons to behave themselves, Hayley supposed it was a natural mistake. But it made her feel stupid all the same.

"Supper's ready," Aunt May announced, tucking her flying grey hair back into its uncoiling loose bun. "You sit here, Hayley, my dear."

Everyone dived for the great table. Chairs squawked on the stone floor and the noise was louder than ever. Harmony and Aunt Alice raced to the kitchen and came back with bowls and casseroles and dishes, while Aunt May bustled behind them with an enormous brown turkey on a huge plate. Aunt May's hair came uncoiled completely as she put the bird down and she had to stand back from the table and pin it up again. Meanwhile Cousin Mercer came back from wherever he had disappeared to and set to work to carve the turkey.

Aunt May was the untidiest person she had ever seen, Hayley thought, sliding nervously into the chair Aunt May had said was hers. Aunt May's clothes were flapping, fraying, overlapping layers of homespun wool, decorated in front by at least three necklaces and a lot of gravy stains. Her feet were in worn out fur slippers, and as for her hair...! Remembering that Cousin Mercer had told her Aunt May was Grandma's eldest daughter, Hayley wondered how on earth Grandma had managed with Aunt May as a child. Grandma always said Hayley was untidy and spent hours trying to make the curly tendrils of Hayley's hair lie flat and neat. "I despair of you, Hayley," Grandma always said. "I really do!" With Aunt May, Grandma must have despaired even more. Still, Hayley thought, looking from neat Aunt Geta to beautiful Aunt Alice, the younger daughters must have pleased Grandma quite a lot.

But Aunt May was kind. She sat next to Hayley and, while Hayley struggled with a plate full of more food than she could possibly eat, Aunt May explained that the Castle had once belonged to Uncle Jolyon, but now it was a guesthouse, except for this one week of the year. "I give the staff a holiday," she said, "and have all the family to stay. Even your Aunt Ellie comes over some years. And of course we have heaps of rooms. I've given you the little room on the half-landing, my dear. I thought you'd feel a little strange if I put you in with the other girls, not being used to it. Just tell me if you're not happy, won't you?"

As Aunt May chatted on in this way, Hayley looked round the table and noticed that Cousin Mercer, sitting behind the remains of the turkey, was the only grown-up man there. *All* the family? she thought. Shouldn't there be some uncles? But she was afraid it might be rude to ask.

The turkey was followed by treacle pudding that Hayley was far too full to eat. While everyone else was devouring it down to the last few sticky golden crumbs, the rain got worse. Hayley could hear it battering on the windows and racing through pipes outside the walls. The Laxton cousins were very put out by it. It seemed that there was some game that they always played when they were at the Castle and they had wanted to start playing it that very evening.

"We couldn't have played tonight anyway," Troy said in his calm way. "It's too dark to see, even if it wasn't raining."

Then the Tigh cousins wanted to know if they could play the game indoors instead. The Laxtons thought this was a splendid notion and said so at the tops of their voices. "We could use the big drawing room for it, couldn't we?" they demanded of Harmony, who seemed to be in charge of the game.

"No way," Harmony said. "It has to be done out of doors. We'll do it tomorrow, when the grass in the paddock has dried."

This raised such a shout of disappointment that Harmony said, "We can do hide-and-seek indoors, if you like."

There were cheers. Aunt Geta murmured, "Bless you, Harmony. Keep them organised till bedtime if you can and we'll let you off clearing the dishes."

So while the aunts cleared away the stacks of plates, everyone except Hayley rushed away into other parts of the house. Aunt May picked up Hayley's suitcase and showed her up a flight of stairs into a small white bedroom with a fluffy bedspread which Hayley much admired. There Aunt May drew the curtains – which flapped and billowed in the gusts of rainy wind outside – and then helped Hayley unpack the suitcase.

"Are these all the clothes you've got, my dear?" Aunt May asked, shaking out the other two floral dresses. "These are not very practical – or very warm."

Hayley felt hugely ashamed. "Grandma said Aunt Ellie was going to buy me clothes in Scotland," she said. "To go to school in."

"Hm," said Aunt May. "I'll have a look and see if I can dig you out something to wear while you're here." She carefully spread Hayley's pink and white pyjamas out over the white bed. "Hm," she said again. "Hayley, if you don't mind my asking, just what *did* you do to make your grandmother so angry?"

Hayley knew she would never be able to explain, when she hardly knew what had happened herself. Aunt May would surely not understand about Flute and Fiddle. Besides, Grandma had never seen either of them. She had only seen the boy with the dogs, but why that had made her so very angry Hayley had no idea. All she could manage to say was, "Grandma said I was romancing at first. Then she said I was bringing the strands *here* and destroying all Grandpa's work. She said Uncle Jolyon wouldn't forgive me for it."

"So she dumps the problem on us," Aunt May said in a harsh, dry voice. "How typical of my mother! As if *we* could stand up to Jolyon any more than she can!

Didn't your grandfather object at all?"

"Yes, but he was upset too," Hayley said. "He said I might grow out of it, but Grandma said I wasn't going to get the chance. She phoned for Cousin Mercer to come and fetch me. She said you'd know what to do."

"*Blowed* if I do!" Aunt May replied. "I'd better ask Geta how she manages, I suppose – or Ellie would be more help. Harmony must have been the same kind of handful when she was younger. Anyway, you run off downstairs and play with the others, and don't bother about it any more."

Hayley would have liked to stay in the small room. It felt safe, even with its creepily billowing curtains. But she had been brought up by Grandma to do as she was told. So she went obediently downstairs and found the big drawing room in the centre of the house. There were at least five doors to this room. Hayley arrived to find cousins rushing in and out, shrieking, while Troy stood in the middle of it with his hands over his eyes, counting to a hundred, and Harmony shouting, "Don't forget! Kitchen's out of bounds and so is the office!"

After that everyone thundered away. Shortly Troy bellowed, "*One hundred!* Coming, ready or not!" and raced away too.

Hayley stood where she was, bewildered again. She had never played this kind of game with lots of people in it and she had no idea what the rules were. She stayed standing there, until Tollie rolled out from under a sofa and looked at her jeeringly.

"You're a wimp," he said, "even for an outcast. And a wuss. And you're not to tell anyone you saw me." And, before Hayley could think of anything to say in reply, Tollie climbed to his feet and hurried out of the nearest door.

Hayley went to sit on a different sofa, beside a very realistic stuffed cat, where she stayed, sadly trying to decide if the stuffed cat was a cushion or a toy, or just an ornament. Being brought up by Grandma and Grandpa simply did not prepare a person for life, she thought.

From time to time, cousins tiptoed through the room, giggling, but none of them took the slightest notice of Hayley. They all know I'm a wimp and an outcast, she thought.

Chapter Two

Hayley was an orphan. All she knew of her parents was the wedding photograph in a silver frame that Grandma propped in the middle of Hayley's bedroom mantelpiece and warned Hayley not to touch. Hayley naturally spent long hours standing on a chair carefully studying the photo. The two people in it looked so happy. Her mother had the same kind of fair good looks as Aunt Alice, except that she seemed more human than Aunt Alice, less perfect. She laughed, with her head thrown back and her veil flying, a lopsided, almost guilty laugh at Hayley's father. He laughed proudly back, proud of Hayley's mother, proud in himself. There was pride in the set of his curly black head, in his gleaming dark eyes and in the way his big brown hand clasped Hayley's mother's white one. He was the one Hayley had her obstinately curly hair and brown complexion from. But, since Hayley's mother was so fair, Hayley's hair had come out a sort of whitish brown and her eyes big and grey. She thought of herself as an exact mixture of both of them and wished with all her strength that they were alive so that she could know them.

Grandma and Grandpa lived in a large house on the edge of London, one of those houses that have a mass of dark shrubs back and front and stained glass in most of the windows, so that it was always rather dark. It had a kitchen part, where a cook and a maid lived. Hayley only ever saw this part when the latest maid took her for walks on the common and they came back in through the kitchen. She was forbidden to go there at any other time in case she disturbed the cook.

The rest of the large dark rooms were mostly devoted to Grandpa's work. Hayley had no idea what

Grandpa's work was, except that it seemed to involve keeping up with the whole world. One entire room was devoted to newspapers and magazines in many languages – most of them the closely-printed, learned kind – and another room was full of maps; maps pinned to walls, piled on shelves in stacks or spread on sloping work benches ready to be studied. The big globe in the middle of this room always fascinated Hayley. The other rooms were crowded to the ceilings with books and strewn with papers, telephones and radios of all colours, except for the room in the basement that was full of computers. The only downstairs room Hayley was officially allowed into was the parlour – and then only if she washed first – where she was allowed to sit in one of its stiff chairs to watch programmes on television that Grandma thought were suitable.

Hayley did not go to school. Grandma gave her lessons upstairs in the schoolroom – which was where Hayley had her meals too – and those lessons were a trial to both of them. Just as Hayley's feathery, flyaway curls continually escaped from Grandma's careful combing and plaiting, so Hayley's attempts to read, write, do sums and paint pictures were always sliding away from the standards Grandma thought correct. Grandma kept a heavy flat ruler on her side of the table with which she rapped Hayley's knuckles whenever Hayley painted outside the lines in the painting book, or wrote something that made her laugh, or got the answer in bags of cheese instead of in money.

Hayley sighed a little as she sat in the Castle drawing-room beside the pretend cat. She had learnt very early on that she could never live up to Grandma's standards. Grandma disapproved of running and shouting and laughing and singing as well as painting outside the lines. Her ideas took in the whole world and Hayley was always overflowing Grandma's edges. It occurred to Hayley now, as she sat on the drawing room sofa, that Grandma must have had four daughters – no, *six*, if you counted Mother and the Aunt Ellie who was in Scotland – and she wondered how on *earth* they had all managed when they were girls.

Luckily, Grandpa was never this strict. Unless he was on a phone to someone important, like Uncle Jolyon or the Prime Minister, he never really minded Hayley sneaking into one of his work rooms. "Are your hands clean?" he would say, looking round from whatever he was doing. And Hayley would nod and smile, knowing this was Grandpa's way of saying she could stay. She smiled now and patted the unreal cat, thinking of her grandfather, huge and bearded, with his round stomach tightly buttoned into a blue-check shirt, turning from his screens to point to a book he had found for her, or to put a cartoon up on another screen for her.

Grandpa was kind, although he never seemed to have much idea what was suitable for small girls. Hayley had several frustrated memories about this. Before she could read, Grandpa had given her a book full of grey drawings of prisons, thinking she would enjoy looking at it. Hayley had not enjoyed it at all. Nor, when she had only just learned to read, had she enjoyed the book called *The Back of the North Wind* which Grandpa had pushed into her hands. The print in it was close and tiny, and Hayley could not understand the story.

But Grandpa had given her many other books later

that she did enjoy. And he often – and quite unpredictably – showed Hayley peculiar things on one or other of his computers. The first time he did this, Hayley was decidedly disappointed. She had been expecting another cartoon, and here Grandpa was, showing her a picture of a large rotating football. Light fell on it sideways as it spun and also fell on the golf ball that was whizzing energetically round the football, going from round to half-lighted to invisible as it whizzed.

"This isn't *Tom and Jerry*," Hayley said.

"No, it's the earth and the moon," Grandpa said. "It's time you learnt what makes day and night."

"But I know that," Hayley objected. "Day is when the sun comes up."

"And I suppose you think the sun goes round the earth?" Grandpa said.

Hayley thought about this. She knew from the globe in the map room that the earth was probably round – though she thought people might well be wrong about that – so it stood to reason that the sun had to circle round it or people in Australia would have night all the time. "Yes," she said.

She was hugely indignant when Grandpa explained that the earth went round the sun, and rather inclined to think Grandpa had got it wrong. Even when Grandpa zoomed the football into the distance and showed her the sun, like a burning beach ball, and the earth circling it along with some peas and several tennis balls, Hayley was by no means convinced. When he told her that it was the earth spinning that made day and night, and the earth circling the sun that made winter and summer, Hayley still thought he might be wrong. Because it was just pictures on a screen, she suspected they were no more real than Donald Duck or Tom and Jerry. And when Grandpa told her that the peas and tennis balls were other planets – Mercury, Venus, Mars, Jupiter, Saturn, Neptune, Pluto – like Earth, and that the tiny things shooting around them in orbits the shape of safety pins were comets, Hayley felt indignant and jealous for Earth, for not being the only one. It took her months to accept that this was the way things were.

She only really accepted it when Grandpa began showing her other things. He showed her the slow growth of Earth from a bare ball of rock, through age-long changes of climate, during which the lands moved about on its surface like leaves floating on a pond, and rocks grew and turned to sand. He showed her dinosaurs and tiny creatures in the sea bed. Then he showed her atoms, molecules and germs – after which Hayley for a long time confused all three with planets going round the sun and, when Grandma insisted that you washed to get rid of germs, wondered if Grandma was trying to clean the universe off her.

Grandpa showed her the universe too, where the Milky Way was like a silver scarf of stars, and other stars floated in shapes that were supposed to be people, swans, animals, crosses and crowns. He also showed Hayley the table of elements, which seemed to her to be something small but heavy, fixed into the midst of all the other floating, spinning, shining strangeness. She thought the elements were probably little number-shaped tintacks that pegged the rest in place.

Grandma had a tendency to object to Grandpa showing Hayley such things. Grandma was liable to march in when Hayley was peacefully settled in front of a cartoon or a plan of the universe and snap the off-button, saying it was not suitable for Hayley to watch. She always went through the books Grandpa gave Hayley too, and took away things like *Fanny Hill* and *The Rainbow* and *Where the Rainbow Ends* and *Pilgrim's Progress*. Hayley never understood quite why these were unsuitable. But the time when Grandma came close to banning all computer displays was when Grandpa showed Hayley the mythosphere.

This was an accident really. It was raining, so that Hayley could not go out for her usual afternoon walk on the common. Grandma went to have her rest. Grandpa had just come home that morning from one of his mysterious absences. Grandpa usually vanished two or three times a year. When Hayley asked where he was, Grandma looked forbidding and answered, "He's gone to visit his other family. Don't be nosy." Grandpa never talked about this at all. When Hayley asked where he had been, he pretended not to hear. But she was always truly glad when he came back. The house felt very dreary without the background hum of the computers and the constant ringing or beeping of all the phones.

So, as soon as Grandma's bedroom door shut, Hayley raced softly downstairs to the computer room.

Grandpa was there, sitting massively in front of a screen, carefully following something on it with a light-pen. Hayley tiptoed up to look over his shoulder. It was a picture of Earth, slowly spinning in dark blue emptiness. She saw Africa rotating past as she arrived. But Africa was quite hard to see because it and the whole globe was swathed in a soft, multicoloured mist. The mist seemed to be made up of thousands of tiny pale threads, all of them moving and swirling outwards. Each thread shone as it moved, gentle and pearly, so the effect was as if Earth spun in a luminous rainbow veil. While Hayley watched, some of the threads wrapped themselves together into a shining skein and this grew on outwards, growing brighter and harder-looking as it grew, and then got thrown gently sideways with the turning of the world, so that it became a silver red spiral. There were dozens of these skeins, when Hayley looked closely, in dozens of silvery colours. But underneath these were thousands of other shining threads which busily drifted and wove and plaited close to Earth.

"That's *beautiful*!" Hayley said. "What are they?"

"Are your hands clean?" Grandpa answered absently. His light-pen steadily picked out a gold gleaming set of threads underneath the spirals and followed it in and out, here and there, through the gauzy mass. He seemed to take it for granted that Hayley had washed her hands because he went on, "This is the mythosphere. It's made up of all the stories, theories and beliefs, legends, myths and hopes, that are generated here on Earth. As you can see, it's constantly growing and moving as people invent new tales to tell or find new things to believe. The older strands move out to become these spirals, where things tend to become quite crude and dangerous. They've hardened off, you see."

"Are they real, the same as atoms and planets?" Hayley asked.

"Quite as real – even realler in some ways," Grandpa replied.

Hayley said the name of it to herself, in order not to forget it. "The mythosphere. And what are you doing with it?"

"Tracing the golden apples," Grandpa said. "Wondering why they've never become a spiral of their own. They mix into other strands all the time. Look." He did something to the keyboard to make Earth turn about and spread itself into a flat plain with continents slowly twirling across it. Golden threads rose from India, from the flatness north of the mountains, from the Mediterranean and from Sweden, Norway and Britain. "See here." Grandpa's big hairy hand pointed the light-pen this way and that as the threads arose. "This thread mingles with three different dragon stories. And this..." the line of light moved southward "...mixes with two quite different stories here. This one's the judgement of Paris and here we have Atalanta, the girl who was distracted from winning a race by some golden apples. And there are hundreds of folk tales..." The pen moved northwards to golden threads growing like grass over Europe and Asia. Grandpa shook his head. "Golden apples all over. They cause death and eternal life and danger and choices. They *must* be important. But none of them combine. None of them spiral and harden. I don't know why."

"If they're real," Hayley said, "can a person go and walk in them, or are they like germs and atoms and too small to see?"

"Oh, yes," Grandpa said, frowning at the threads. "Only I don't advocate walking in the spirals. Everything gets pretty fierce out there."

"But nearer in. Do you walk or float?" Hayley wanted to know.

"You could take a boat if you want," Grandpa said, "or even a car sometimes. But I prefer to walk myself. It's—"

But here Grandma came storming in and seized Hayley by one arm. "Really! Honest to goodness, Tas!" she said, dragging Hayley away from the screen. "You ought to know better than to let Hayley in among this stuff!"

"It's not doing her any harm!" Grandpa protested.

"On the contrary. It could do immense harm – to us and Hayley too, if Jolyon gets to hear of it!" Grandma retorted. She dragged Hayley out of the room and shut the door with a bang. "Hayley, you are not to have anything to do with the mythosphere *ever* again!" she said. "Forget you ever saw it!"

Chapter Three

Being ordered to forget about the mythosphere was like being ordered not to think of a blue elephant. Hayley could not forget those beautiful swirling, drifting, shining threads. She thought about the mythosphere constantly, almost as often as she stood on a chair and stared at the young, happy faces in her parents' wedding photo. It was if the mythosphere had cast a spell on her. Something tugged at her chest whenever she remembered it and she felt a great sad longing that was almost like feeling sick.

It was a few days later that she met the musicians

properly for the first time. Hayley was never sure whether or not the mythosphere had anything to do with it. But it seemed likely that it did.

She knew one of the musicians by sight anyway. She saw him every time the latest maid took her round by the shops instead of out on the common. Martya, the newest maid, always nodded and smiled at him. Martya was a big strong girl with hair like the white silk fringes on Grandma's parlour furniture – soft, straight hair that was always swirling across her round pink face. Unfortunately, Martya's face did not live up to her beautiful hair in any way. Grandma sniffed and called Martya "distressingly plain", and then sighed and wished Martya spoke better English. When she sent Martya and Hayley round by the shops, Grandma always had to give Martya a list written in big capital letters because Martya didn't read English very well either. This, Grandma explained to Hayley, was because Martya was from Darkest Russia, where they used different letters as well as different language. It was Martya's bad English that first caused Hayley's interest in the musician.

He was very tall and skinny and he always wore a dark suit with a blue scarf tucked in around the neck. He had stood for as long as Hayley could remember, rain or shine, in the exact same place outside the pub called The Star, playing high sweet notes on a shabby little violin that looked much too small for him. The case of the violin lay open on the pavement by his feet and people occasionally chucked coppers or 5p's into it as they passed. Hayley always wondered why he never seemed to play any real tunes – just music, she thought of it.

Neither Hayley nor Martya ever had any coins to drop into the case, but Martya never failed to nod and smile at the man; whereupon he nodded back, violin and all, still playing away, and a large beaming smile would spread up his thin face, making his eyes gleam the same bright blue as his scarf. Up till then Hayley had always assumed he was old. But he had such a young smile that she now noticed that his hair, under the round black cap he always wore, was not *old* white, but the same sort of fine white hair as Martya's.

"Is he some relation of yours?" she asked. "Is that why you nod?"

"No. Is polite," Martya said. "He is musician."

The way she said it, it sounded like "magician". Hayley said, "Oh!" very impressed, and from then on she too nodded and smiled at the musician, with considerable awe. And he always smiled back.

Hayley longed to ask the musician about his magic powers, but Martya always hurried her past to the shops before she had a chance to ask.

Then one afternoon they were in the corner shop just beyond The Star – where Hayley could still hear the violin in the distance, so sad and sweet that she felt herself aching with the same longing she felt about the mythosphere – when Martya fell into an argument with Mr Ahmed who ran the shop. Both of them pointed to Grandma's list and Mr Ahmed kept saying, "No, no, I assure you, this word is orangeade." While Martya said, over and over, "Is *oranges* we need!"

Hayley waited for them to stop, idly kicking at the base of the ice-cream machine while she waited. And something tinkled beside her shoe. She looked down and saw it was a pound coin.

Without even having to think, she snatched it up

and raced out of the shop, round the bulging steps of The Star, back to where the musician stood playing. There she dropped the coin into the violin case and waited breathlessly in front of him.

After a moment he seemed to realise that she wanted something. He took his bow off his violin and the violin down from his chin. "Thank you," he said.

He had a nice, light kind of voice. Much encouraged by it, Hayley blurted out, "Please, I just wanted to know, are you a magician?"

He thought about it. "It depends what you mean by magician," he said at length. "My ways are not your ways. But I have a brother who stands in the sun, who could tell you more."

Hayley looked across the street, where the sunlight blazed on shoppers and glinted off shop windows. She had often vaguely wondered why the musician always stood here, on the shady side of the street. She turned back to ask if the brother was a musician as well.

But here Martya dashed up in a panic and seized Hayley's arm. "You don't go, you don't go! Your baba kills me! So sorry," she gasped at the musician. "She bother you."

He smiled his blue-eyed smile. "Not at all," he said.

Martya gave him a flustered glare and dragged Hayley back to the shop, where she and Mr Ahmed had settled the argument by getting Grandma both oranges *and* orangeade. Grandma was not pleased when they got home. She had wanted orange juice.

Thereafter, whenever they went to the shops, Hayley always tried to tempt Martya to walk on the sunny side of the street, in hopes of meeting the musician's brother. Martya nodded and smiled as if she quite understood, and then stayed on the usual side of the road. Nodding and smiling turned out to be a habit with Martya. She used it instead of understanding English. She used it particularly when Grandma told her to clean the silver or sweep the stairs. Grandma soon began saying Martya was a lazy slattern.

"Now let us see," Grandma said, one afternoon a few days later, "if you can manage to do one simple thing, Martya. No, don't nod, don't smile. Just look at Hayley's shoes." She pointed. Martya and Hayley both looked down at Hayley's neat black shiny shoes. "Now go to the shoe shop," Grandma said, "with this note and this money, and get Hayley another pair just the same but half a size larger. Can you do that?"

"I can do that, Grandma," Hayley said joyfully. The shoe shop was on the sunny side of the street.

"I'm talking to Martya," Grandma said. "Martya is doing the buying. I want the same kind exactly, Martya. No other colour, no fancy bits. Have you understood?"

Martya nodded and smiled vigorously and the pair of them set off towards the shops. On the way, Martya said, rather helplessly, "I don't know how is shoes. What is fancy bits?"

"I'll show you," Hayley said.

The shoe shop was quite a long way down the road from The Star, where the musician was playing as usual. Hayley waved to him across the street, but she was not sure he saw her. When they reached the shoe shop, Hayley led Martya in front of the window and pointed to the various different shoes inside it. "Look – those pink ones with cowboy fringes have the fancy bits, and so do those with a flower on front. Do you see?"

While Martya pulled her hair aside in order to bend down and stare at the shoes, and then did her usual nodding and smiling, Hayley suddenly began hearing sweet distant snatches of music. It was not violin music. She was not sure what instrument it was, but it flowed and stopped and flowed again, in some of the loveliest sounds she had ever heard. "It's his brother," she said to Martya. Martya just nodded and smiled and looked at shoes. Hayley said, "I'll be back in a minute," and walked sideways away along the fronts of the shops, tracking the music. "Like the Pied Piper or something," she said aloud, as the sounds led her on, and on, and then round a corner into a small side street.

The musician was there, standing in blazing sunlight and, to Hayley's delight, he was actually playing a pipe, the kind you held sideways out along one shoulder to play. Hayley dimly thought it might be a flute. She had never heard such lovely sounds as those that came pouring out of it, although she did wish that he would keep to one tune, instead of playing in snatches. One moment he would be playing something wild and jolly. Then he would break off and start another tune, this one melting and sad. Then it would be music you could march to. She stood and surveyed him and rejoiced.

He had hair like Martya's, quite long, but not as long as Martya's, that blew around his head in fine white strands, and he was as tall and thin as the violin-player, though nothing like so neat. His clothes were green and baggy, and a green, green scarf fluttered from his neck. A baggy green hat lay on the ground by his bare feet, waiting for money.

He was watching Hayley watching him while he played. His eyes were the same green as his scarf. Hayley had never seen eyes that colour before, nor had she ever looked into eyes that were so direct and interested and kind. It was as if he and Hayley knew one another already.

"I'm sorry I haven't any money," she said.

You couldn't play a flute and talk. He took the flute away from his mouth to smile and say, "That doesn't matter."

"Are you the violin man's brother?" she asked.

"That's right," he said. "Who are you?"

"I'm Hayley Foss," Hayley said. "What are you called?"

He grinned, the same sort of youthful grin as his brother's, and asked, "What do you want to call me?"

All sorts of names flooded through Hayley's mind, so many that she was surprised into taking a deep, gasping breath. "Flute," she said, in the end.

He laughed. "That'll do. And I suppose that makes my brother's name Fiddle. One of us had better warn him. What can I do for you?"

"Are you a magician?" Hayley asked.

"In many ways, yes," he said. "I don't live by the usual rules."

"*I* have to live by rules all the time," Hayley said wistfully. "Can you show me some magic?"

Flute looked at her consideringly – and quite sympathetically, she thought. He seemed to be going to agree, but then he looked up over Hayley's head and said, " Some other time, perhaps."

Martya was rushing up the small street, waving a pair of large pink shoes with cowboy fringes, and a lady from the shoe shop was rushing after her. Martya was so agitated at losing Hayley that she forgot to speak English at all and shouted a torrent of her own language, while the shop lady kept saying, "I don't care where you come from. You haven't paid for those shoes."

Flute twisted up one side of his face, so that half of it seemed to be smiling at Hayley and the other half looking seriously at the shop lady, and said, "I think I'd better sort this out for you." He said to the lady, "It's all right. She thought this little girl had gone missing, you see." Then he spoke to Martya in what was clearly her own language.

Martya replied with a gush of Darkest Russian, clapping the pink shoes together in front of her bosom, as a substitute for wringing her hands. They were very big shoes, much more Martya's size than Hayley's. Flute spoke to her soothingly while he collected his hat and shut his flute into a long case. By the time they were all walking back to the shoe shop, he was wearing rather battered green boots that Hayley had certainly not seen him put on.

He *did* do some magic! Hayley thought. Quite a lot

of it! she added to herself, as she watched Flute calming everyone in the shop down and making sure that Martya counted out enough of Grandma's money to pay for the large pink shoes. Then he smiled at Hayley, said, "I'll see you," and left.

Martya and Hayley went home, where Grandma was far from pleased. Hayley said repeatedly, "It wasn't her fault, or Flute's, Grandma. They both thought you meant the shoes were for *her*." While Martya nodded and smiled and hugged the shoes happily.

"Be quiet, Hayley," Grandma snapped. "Martya, I have had enough of this nodding and smiling. It's just an excuse for laziness and dishonesty. You'll have to leave. Now."

Martya's ugly face contorted inside her beautiful hair. "Laziness I am?" she said to Grandma. "Then of you, what? You do nothing all day but give orders and make rules! I go and pack now – and take my shoes!" She went stumping up the stairs, scowling. "Your baba is a monster!" she said as she stamped past Hayley. "You I pity from the depths of my chest!"

It startled Hayley. She had not thought of Grandma

as a monster – she had just thought life was like that: long and boring and full of rules and things you mustn't do. Now here was Martya actually pitying her for it. She wondered if it made sense.

But there were no more walks, to the shops or out on the common, for a while after that. Until a new maid was found to clean things and take Hayley out in the afternoons, Hayley was sent into the back garden instead. There she wandered about among the dark, crowding laurel bushes, thinking about her parents, longing for the mythosphere and wondering if Grandma really was a monster. Sometimes, when she was right in the midst of the laurels and knew she could not be seen from any of the windows, she crouched down – careful not to get her knees dirty – and secretly built bowers out of twigs, castles made of pebbles and gardens from anything she could find. "Mythosphere things," she called them to herself.

She was building a particularly elaborate rock garden about a week later, made of carefully piled gravel and ferns, when she looked up to see Flute standing among the laurels with his hands in his pockets. He was staring up at the house as if he was wondering about it. Hayley could not think how Flute had got in. There was a high brick wall round the garden and no way in except through the house.

"Hallo," she said. "What are you doing here?"

Flute had obviously not known she was there. He whirled round, thoroughly startled, and his green scarf blew tastefully out among his hair. "Oh," he said. "I didn't see you. I was wondering what went on in this house."

"Nothing much does," Hayley told him, rather dryly. "Grandpa works and Grandma makes rules."

Flute frowned and shook his head slightly. The green scarf fluttered. His eyes stared into Hayley's, green and steady. "I know you," he said. "You were with the Russian lady and the shoes."

"Martya. She left," Hayley said.

"That doesn't surprise me," Flute said. "This house isn't for the likes of her. Why are you in it?"

"I'm an orphan," Hayley explained. "They bring me up." Flute nodded, taking this in, and then smiled at her, with some little doubtful creases beside his mouth. Hayley found herself adoring him, in a way she never adored even Grandpa. "How did you get in here?" she said. "Over the wall?"

Flute shook his head. "I don't do walls," he said. "I'll show you, if you'll just follow me for a few steps." He turned and walked, with a soft clatter of leaves, in among the laurel trees.

Hayley sprang up from her rock garden – it was finished anyway – and followed the swishing and the glimpses of green scarf among the dark leaves. There had to be a gate in the wall that she had never found. But she never saw the wall. She followed Flute out of the laurels into a corner of the common. Really the common. She saw cars on the road in the distance and Grandpa's familiar red house in the row beyond the road. "Good heavens!" she said, and looked up at Flute with respect. "That's more magic, isn't it? Can you show me some *more* more?"

Flute thought about it. "What do you want to see?"

There was no question about that. "The mythosphere," Hayley said.

Flute was rather taken aback. He put his hands into his baggy pockets and looked down at her seriously.

"Are you sure? Someone *has* warned you, have they, that things in the mythosphere are often harder and – well – fiercer than they are here?"

Hayley nodded. "Grandpa said the strands harden off when they get further out."

"All right," Flute said. "We'll take a look at some of the nearest parts then. It'll have to be just a short look, because I wasn't expecting to see you and I have things to do today. Follow me then."

Chapter Four

Flute turned and strode back among the laurels, green scarf streaming. Hayley pattered after him in the greatest excitement. Not much happened at first, except that they came out into proper woodland where paths seemed to run in several directions. Flute looked this way and that and finally chose a path that was lightly strewn with brown and yellow autumn leaves. After a short way, the leaves were in thick drifts and the trees overhead were yellow and brown and apricot, and rattled in a sad, small autumn breeze. Hayley – and Flute too – began to enjoy shuffling the leaves into heaps and then kicking them, until Flute put a hand out for Hayley to stop.

Someone was coming along a path that crossed theirs, whistling merrily.

Hayley stood nearly knee deep in leaves and watched a splendid young man go striding past, crunching coloured leaves under his sandals. He was obviously a hunter. His main clothing was a big spotted leopardskin that draped over one shoulder and fastened around his hips to make a sort of skirt, and he carried an enormous longbow almost as tall as himself. The arrows for it hung in a long leather box over his left shoulder. His muscles bulged and gleamed. Grandma would have called him a dirty savage, but to Hayley he looked neat and crisp, like an actor dressed up as a hunter for a film. She could see that his neat little beard and his chestnut curls were shining and clean.

"Who is he?" she whispered.

"Orion," Flute whispered back. "He's a hunter."

There seemed to be a group of ladies in long dresses suddenly, in among the trees. The hunter stopped whistling, peered, and whipped an arrow, long and wickedly sharp, out from his arrow-holder. Then, holding it ready beside his bow, he broke into a fast, striding run. The ladies all screamed and ran away.

Hayley did not blame them. "Can't he *see* they're not animals?" she said.

"Not always," Flute said, as hunter and ladies all disappeared among the trees.

Flute and Hayley turned a corner and came out beside a lake then, where it seemed to be nearly winter. All the trees and bushes around the bleak little stretch of water were brown and almost empty of leaves. A young lady in a white dress came down the bank towards the shore. When she was right beside the water, she looked around, grinning mischievously, and crouched down. Her white dress melted into her all over and she was suddenly a swan. Off she launched, white and stately, and sailed across the lake.

Hayley saw a hunter then. She thought he was not the same hunter as the first one, but it was hard to be sure. He was in dark clothes, but he had the same sort of huge bow and a case of arrows. He was coming stealthily down to the lakeside with an arrow ready beside his bow. When he saw the swan lady, he put the arrow in the bow, raised it and, very slowly and carefully, drew the arrow back until the bow was a great arc.

Hayley cried out, "Oh no! *Don't*!"

The hunter did not seem to hear her. He let the arrow fly. Out in the lake, the swan collapsed into a white, spouting turmoil.

"Let's move on," Flute said sadly. He took Hayley's hand and pulled her away from the lakeside. But before the bushes hid the lake, Hayley *had* to look back. She saw the hunter wading in the water, dragging the white floppy shape of the lady to the shore. He seemed to be crying his eyes out.

The next part they went through had swans in it everywhere. Three swans with crowns on their heads glided on a sudden sea. A group of young women ran down to the beach a bit further on and then took off as swans in a white beating of huge wings. More wings beat and some swans came in to land beside a big bonfire. As they landed, they turned into young men. This happened several times. Sometimes there was just one swan, sometimes a whole flock. Then Flute and Hayley arrived at a place where a young woman timidly held out her hand to a huge swan, as big as she was. There was something about that big swan that Hayley did not like at all.

"I think," Flute said, "that we'll take another strand now. All right?" When Hayley nodded, he turned off along a way that was greener, where the sun shone among forest trees that seemed to be putting out new spring leaves.

They passed through a sunny clearing where golden midges circled under a big oak tree. When Hayley looked at the midges closely, they were very small winged people. She cried out with pleasure.

"More like it, eh?" Flute said, grinning.

The midge people all flew away as he said it. They seemed to have been frightened by a growing noise, over to the left. It was a sound of yelping, pattering and panting. Shortly a whole crowd of dogs burst into the clearing, excited, long-legged hunting dogs with their tongues hanging out. Hayley could see that they were all little more than puppies. They saw Hayley and

Flute and rushed towards them, so that in seconds they were surrounded by curved, waving tails, big floppy ears and wide panting mouths with long pink tongues draping out of them. One puppy reared up to put both paws on Flute's stomach. Flute laughed and rubbed its ears. Hayley, a little timidly, stroked the head of the nearest hound. This caused all the rest to clamour for attention too. Hayley had to laugh. It was like being in a warm, boisterous bath, full of excitement and affection.

A boy came panting into the clearing, trailing a long whip. He stopped and laughed when he saw them surrounded in happy dogs. "Sorry," he said. "I'm trying to teach them to follow a scent. You wouldn't believe how easily they get distracted!" He was a good looking boy, not much older than Hayley, and he seemed as happy and excited as his dogs. He cracked his whip in the air. "Down, Chaser! Come *on*, Snuffer! Bell and Doom, get away, get *on*!" He cracked his whip again. Hayley saw that he was careful not to hit any of the dogs. "Come *on*, all of you!" he shouted.

It took a while, and a lot more shouting and whip

cracking, but at length the dogs turned away from these interesting new humans they had found. One or two put noses to the ground. One gave an excited yelp. And finally they all rushed away into the forest with the boy running and bounding behind them.

"Oh, I *liked* him!" Hayley said. "Who is he?"

"Another huntsman," Flute said. "One of many. We're on the hunters' strand here. But I think we ought to be getting back now. I've got a busy afternoon and I suspect that your grandmother will be wanting you by now." He strode off through the sunlit forest in the same direction that the boy and his dogs had gone.

Hayley said, "Bother!" as she trudged after him. The midge people had come back again to circle in the sun and she had wanted to watch them.

Just as she caught up with Flute, the boy came racing back towards them. He was older now, with a little curl of beard on his chin, and he ran as if he was running for his life. If he noticed Flute or Hayley as he tore past them, he gave no sign of it. His eyes were set with terror and he just ran. Behind him came all the dogs, older too now, and a bit gaunt and grizzled. They were all snarling. One or two had foam coming from their mouths and all their eyes glared. As the boy crashed past Flute and Hayley the foremost dog almost caught him and then lost ground because it had a bloodstained piece of the boy's trousers in its mouth. The rest chased on furiously.

Hayley clutched Flute's hand. "Do they catch him?"

Flute nodded. "I'm afraid so."

Hayley was horrified. "*Why*?"

"He managed to be really offensive to a goddess," Flute told her. "Things like this happen on every strand, you know. The mythosphere is not an entirely happy place."

"But it looks so beautiful!" Hayley protested.

Flute laughed a little. "Beauty isn't made of sugar," he said. "Through this way now."

They pushed their way through some thick laurels and came out into the common again. Hayley stared from the bushes behind to her to the still impossible sight of her grandparents' house beyond the road, *over there.*

Flute said, "Do you think you can find your own way back, or do you want me to take you?"

"I'd rather stay with you," Hayley said. She felt raw with sorrow over the fate of the nice boy.

"Not possible, I'm afraid," Flute said. "But I'll show you some more magic quite soon if you like. See you." He plunged back among the laurels and was gone.

Definitely gone, Hayley knew. She stood and wondered what Grandma might say if Hayley simply went across the road and rang the doorbell, and Grandma opened the door. It hardly bore thinking of. No, she had to get back to the garden somehow.

She pushed her way dubiously in among the laurels. And pushed and rustled and plunged and rattled, and for a while wondered if she was going to have to just stand there and yell for help, or even stay in the bushes for ever. Then she was quite suddenly through them and into the garden, almost treading on her rock garden. She was about to kick it moodily to bits – it was only a heap of stones with wilting ferns stuck in it, and that nice boy was being ripped apart by his own dogs – when she heard Grandma calling her. At which Hayley forgot that she was not supposed to run and rushed frantically up the path to the garden door.

"I think Flute is an ancient supernatural being," she panted unwisely to Grandma.

"Oh, just *look* at you!" Grandma exclaimed. "How *did* you get so untidy?"

"In the bushes. Flute is just what I call him because I don't know his real name," Hayley babbled. "He has a green scarf and hair like Martya's."

Grandma stiffened. "Will you stop romancing this instant, Hayley! Uncle Jolyon's here. He wants to see you for tea in the parlour. If it wasn't for that, I'd send you to bed without supper for telling stories. Go and comb your hair and put on a clean dress this moment. I want you back downstairs and looking respectable in ten minutes! So hurry!"

Hayley sobered up. She saw she had been stupid to mention Flute to Grandma. Flute was – if ever anyone was – a person who overflowed Grandma's boundaries. Flute didn't do walls. And Grandma did walls all the time, Hayley thought as she scurried away down the passage to the stairs. She was halfway up the stairs when she heard Grandpa and Uncle Jolyon coming out of the map room, arguing. It was funny, she thought, peeping over the banisters, the way unusual things always seemed to happen in clusters. Uncle Jolyon only visited here about once a year and when he did, Grandpa was always very, very polite to him. But now Grandpa was shouting at him.

"You just watch yourself!" Grandpa bellowed. "Any more of this control-freak nonsense and I shall walk away! *Then* where will you be?"

As Hayley scudded on upwards, Uncle Jolyon was making peace-keeping sort of noises. She took another peep at them on the next turn of the stairs. They were both big, stout men, but where Grandpa was grey, Uncle Jolyon had a fine head of curly white hair and a white beard and moustache to go with it. He backed away as Grandpa positively roared, "*Oh yes, I can do it!* I did it before and you didn't like it one bit, did you?"

"Hayley!" Grandma called. "Are you changed yet?"

Hayley called out, "Nearly, Grandma!" and pelted on up to her room. There she flung off her grubby dress, flung on a new one and managed to make her hair lie flat by pasting it down with the water she scrubbed her muddy knees in. Then she went demurely down to the parlour, where Grandma was pouring tea and Grandpa and Uncle Jolyon were drinking it, all smiles, as if neither of them had just been quarrelling in the hall.

Nobody took much notice of Hayley. She sat on an embroidered chair nibbling at a hard rock cake – which made her feel like a rather small squirrel – and listened to the three adults talk about world affairs, and science, and the stock market, and some prehistoric carvings someone had found in a cave near Nottingham. If Uncle Jolyon had specially wanted to see Hayley, he showed few signs of it. He only looked at her once. Hayley was struck then at how dishonest the crinkles round his eyes made him look. She thought it must be because she had just seen Flute. Flute's green eyes looked at you direct and straight, without any disguising of his feelings. Uncle Jolyon's eyes calculated and concealed things. Hayley found she distrusted him very much.

When the tea was drunk, Uncle Jolyon leaned over, grunting a little, and pinched Hayley's chin. "You be a good girl now," he said to her, "and do what your grandparents say."

The way he smiled, full of false kindness and hidden meanings, truly grated on Hayley. *And* the pinch hurt. "Why are you so dishonest?" she said.

Grandma went stiff as a post. Grandpa seemed to curl up a little, as if he expected someone to hit him. Uncle Jolyon, however, leant his head back and laughed heartily.

"Because I have to be," he said. "Nobody expects a businessman to be *honest*, child." And he shouted with laughter again.

Uncle Jolyon went away after that – with Grandpa seeing him into his waiting taxi in the friendliest possible way – and Hayley was left to face Grandma's anger.

"How *dare* you be so rude to poor Uncle Jolyon!" she said. "Go up to your room and *stay* there! I don't want to set eyes on you until you've remembered how to behave properly."

Hayley was quite glad to go. She wanted to be alone to digest all the things she had seen that afternoon. But she could not resist turning round halfway upstairs. "Uncle Jolyon isn't poor," she said. "And he orders Grandpa around."

"*Go!*" Grandma commanded, pointing a strong finger upstairs.

Hayley went. She went into her room and sat there for a long time, staring at the photo of her parents on the mantelpiece. So happy. That was what Hayley had expected the mythosphere to be like, full of happiness, but it seemed to be full of tragic things instead.

After a while, though, it occurred to her that in a way it *was* full of happiness. The hunter in the leopardskin had been happy, until he saw the ladies and turned all mean. The ladies who turned into swans had been happy as they ran down to the water. And that boy with the dogs had been happiest of all until he was stupid enough to annoy a goddess.

"It's *silly* to let the bad things come out on top!" Hayley said aloud. "The good, happy things are just as important. They just don't seem to last. You want to catch them at their best and keep them if you can."

She looked hard at the photo and wished she had another photo to put beside it, of the boy and his dogs. They had been having such fun chasing through the budding green woods. She began to imagine them, not as she had seen them, but before that, running in an eager line, with the boy at the back of them, cracking his whip and laughing at their mistakes. She remembered that each dog was slightly different from the others. Snuffer had one brown ear. Chaser was all white, while Doom was nearly black, with yellow speckles. Bell had a pale brown patch, like a saddle, on her back. The brown-and-yellow one was Pickles, the one with the white ears was Flags and the other dark-coloured one was Genius. Then there were Rags, Noser, Wag and Petruvia, all of whom were greyish with black bits in different places. As for the boy, he had been wearing baggy clothes rather like Flute's, only in brighter colours, blues and reds. His whip had red patterns on the handle.

Hayley could really almost *see* them, rushing along, tails up and waving. She could hear their pattering and panting, the occasional yelp, and the boy laughing as he cracked his whip. She could smell dog and leafy forest. So happy–

Grandma came in just then, saying, "Well? Have you remembered– *Hayley*!"

Hayley came to herself with a jump to find the boy

and his dogs really and truly rushing through her room in front of her, soundless now and fading as they ran, while Grandma stared at them in grey outrage.

"I have had enough of you, Hayley," Grandma said. "You're a wicked little girl – quite uncontrollable! Haven't I taught you not mix There with Here?"

The dogs faded silently away and the boy melted off after them. Hayley turned miserably to Grandma. "They were happy. They weren't doing any harm."

"If that's all you can say—" Grandma began.

"It is," Hayley interrupted defiantly. "It's what I say. *Happy*!"

Chapter Five

Hayley hated to remember the next bit. Grandma refused to explain or speak to Hayley. She simply rammed Hayley's clothes into a suitcase and made Grandpa phone Aunt May to send Cousin Mercer to fetch Hayley away. Hayley was locked into her room until Cousin Mercer arrived the following morning and nobody came near her, even to bring food. That was bad enough. So was the journey that followed, long and confusing and full of delays and rain. But the worst was that Hayley was sure that Flute would turn up in the garden and find her gone, and be terribly puzzled. She was sure she would never see Flute again.

She sat beside the pretend cat, trying not to think at all. She could hear the running and shouting again in the distance but it did not seem very important.

For a moment, she thought she was crying. Drops were falling heavily on the pretend cat and then splashing on to her leg. It was only when more drops fell on her head that Hayley realised the water must be coming from somewhere else. She looked up. The ceiling above her sofa was covered in upside-down puddles, with big dewy yellow drops forming in the middle of them and then plopping down. At almost the moment when she turned her face up, the puddles all became too big to hold together and water began coming down in streams, nearly as hard as it was raining outside.

Hayley jumped up. "Oh dear," she said, collecting cushions and the pretend cat and dumping them into a dry chair. She tried to push the sofa out from under the flood, but it was too heavy for her to move. She simply got sprayed with water splattering up off the carpet. "I think I'd better tell someone," she said doubtfully.

She ran out into the hall. No one seemed to be about down there, but there was a lot of shouting and running about going on somewhere upstairs. Hayley rather timidly climbed the stairs, past the small safe room she had been given and on up to the right.

A river of water met her near the top, coming down like a waterfall from stair to stair. The landing, when she came to it, was a small oblong lake, and the corridor off to the right, which must have been right above the lounge, was a dark tunnel filled with rain. Someone screamed, "Turn off that light! It's *dangerous*!" Footsteps thundered and splashed somewhere out of sight, and voices from unseen cousins and aunts yelled, "Tollie! Where *are* you? We *need* you!" and "Bring that bucket here, *quick*!" and "Throw all the towels down there!" and in between, everyone yelled for Tollie again.

"I think they know," Hayley said to herself. She stood to the side of the waterfall at the top of the stairs, wondering what she ought to do.

Aunt May and Troy, both of them soaking wet, burst out from the rain in the dark corridor and splashed to a stop when they saw Hayley.

"*She'll* do!" Troy cried out. "She's a lot smaller than Tollie."

"Oh, so she will!" Aunt May gasped. Sheets of water sprayed round her wet slippers as she dived on Hayley and took hold of her arm. "*Do* you mind helping us, dear? One of the gutters is blocked and we're all too big to get out of the window."

Troy seized Hayley's other arm and the two of them towed her across the landing. The lake soaked Hayley's shoes and socks instantly. She was rather surprised to find that the water was not really cold. But then the whole of Ireland was not really as cold as London.

"Mercer's tried getting to it from outside with a ladder," Troy explained, switching on the big electric torch he was carrying, "but the wind blew him down, so it has to be unblocked by someone small enough to get out through the top bathroom window."

"*Will* you do that for us, dear?" Aunt May said as they all plunged into the downpour inside the corridor. "We'll hang on to you. You'll be quite safe."

"Yes," Hayley said, "of course," thinking that there didn't seem to be much choice.

"Of *course* you will!" Troy said warmly.

With rain thumping and pattering on their heads and backs, the three of them rushed up a flight of stairs that was exactly like a waterfall, to where Troy's torch glinted on choppy waves in another flooded corridor. Dark shapes of people churned about in it, shouting to one another to "Keep that door *shut*!" and then, "Where *is* Tollie?"

Aunt May and Troy wheeled sideways from here and pounded up another flight of stairs which were – confusingly – completely dry. Both of them yelled over their shoulders, "It's all right. We don't need Tollie. We've got Hayley instead!" and then wheeled sideways again into a little bathroom with a sloping ceiling. Someone had put a big flickering lantern in the washbasin there. By its light, Hayley saw a bath wedged in under the slope of the ceiling and above the bath a small square skylight propped open on a thin metal bar. Rain was spattering viciously in through the opening. Hayley looked up at it and thought, How do I get up *there*?

"Don't worry, we'll lift you," Troy said. He picked up a bath stool and banged it down in the bath. "Hop up there and I'll boost you," he said.

Before Hayley could move, Aunt May scrambled into the bath, saying, "I'll keep it steady." Whereupon her sopping slippers shot out from under her and she sat down with a splash, sending the stool clanging into the bath taps.

"Oh, not *again*, Auntie!" Troy said. He put his shoulder under Aunt May's waving arm and helped her flounder to her feet again. Somehow, in the course of the vast scrambling that followed, Aunt May's necklace burst. Beads clattered into the bath and rolled about on the dimly lit floor. "Last necklace to go," Troy said cheerfully. "Don't tread on a bead, Hayley. The floor's covered with them now." He put the stool back under the skylight and squelched into the bath beside it. He held out both hands to Hayley. "Up you get," he said. "Take my torch and get on the stool."

"You'll need the torch to see the drain," Aunt May

panted. Her hair was now out of whatever had held it together and fanned over her big shoulders like a lion's mane. "The drain's down to the left of the window."

Hayley took hold of the torch and found herself being hauled up on to the stool. She stood there, wobbling rather, feeling Troy grab her from one side and Aunt May from the other, and cautiously took the metal bar off its spike and pushed the tiny window open with her head.

It was horrible out there. Windy rain stormed into her face. Worse still, when she worked the torch through beside her face and got it pointed downwards, all she could see was a sort of trench full of turbulent water just below her and the square shapes of the castle parapet beyond that. The drain was obviously deep under water. She was going to have to guess where it was. The only way Hayley could see to get near it was to ooze herself out of the window headfirst. And then grope.

"We've got you," Troy said encouragingly as Hayley began to wriggle herself forward.

The frame of the skylight was only just big enough

for her to get through. As Hayley wriggled onward, the spike that the metal bar hooked on to scraped its way agonisingly down the middle of her chest, while the bar itself hung down and poked her in the head. By the time her feet had left the stool and she was hanging half in and half out, she was still a foot away from the murky ditch of water and being stabbed in the tummy button by the spike. She was going to have to get all of her outside.

Behind her, she could hear the little bathroom filling up with people. Someone said, "She'll never get to it like that!"

Oh yes I *will*! Hayley thought. "Be ready to hold my feet!" she shouted and thought she heard someone say "OK." Then, clutching the torch in her right hand, she began to inch herself down the sloping tiles outside. Rain pelted across her. Before long, she had the feeling it was raining *upwards* into her pants. The skylight bit into her shins, the tiles scraped her front. The only comforting thing was that she could feel Troy's hands warm and strong on her left leg and Aunt May's hands, softer but just as strong, holding her right calf.

They were paying her out of the window like a rope.

The hands had reached her ankles before Hayley could even touch the water. Left, she thought. She had to stretch and ooze and extend herself sideways before her hand could go into the rippling flood. It was surprisingly un-cold to her fingers. The hands were holding her shoes by then. And she stretched and oozed and tried to lengthen herself again, until finally her fingertips met a rough, leaded bottom. She couldn't feel any kind of drain. Rather desperately, she swished her hand further to the left. Here there was the faintest feeling that the water was pulling at her fingers. Almost shrieking with the effort, she managed to move her hand that way.

The tips of her fingers touched something thick and rubbery-feeling. With another desperate stretch, Hayley somehow got one finger under it, and then her thumb on top. Then she could pick whatever-it-was up.

It came up with a gurgle. Hayley was so surprised at how quickly things happened then that she nearly screamed. Water thundered past her nose from right to left and tried to take her hair with it. To the left, it became a whirlpool, fairly whizzing round and round, and gargled away down the unblocked drain so fast that by the time Troy and Aunt May, thoroughly alarmed at the noises Hayley was making, had started to haul on her ankles, the gutter was empty.

Troy and Aunt May went on hauling. Hayley scraped rapidly and painfully up over the tiles, and agonisingly across the spike, and landed on the stool in the bath again, soaking wet and with her dress torn completely open down the middle.

Someone shouted, "She *did* it!"

There were cheers from the crowded bathroom behind her. Someone else said, "What was it? What *is* she holding?"

Blinking in the lantern light, Hayley turned herself around on the stool. Cousins and aunts were packed into the tiny space, dimly lit and staring, with Cousin Mercer ducking his wet head in through the door at the back and Tollie squashed up against the bath in front. Troy gently prised the torch out of Hayley's right hand and switched it off. Aunt May seized Hayley's left wrist. "Good heavens!" she said.

Hayley looked that way to find that her fingers were clamped round a pork chop. It was large. It was raw, and whitish with waterlogging, and sort of triangular, but there was no doubt what it was. It was almost exactly the right size and shape to block a drain.

"It's a pork chop!" Aunt Alice exclaimed. "However did *that* get into the gutter?"

Hayley looked at Tollie, down near her soaking shoes, and knew at once. If ever she saw guilt and annoyance, it was in Tollie's face at that moment. No doubt Tollie had hoped to be the one who went heroically out through the window. But when Aunt May said, "We have crows and seagulls here all the time – one of them must have dropped it," Hayley did not contradict her. Even though Tollie looked up at her with scorn and dislike, for being too feeble to tell, Hayley did not say a word. She was shivering all over and her front hurt.

Aunt Celia said, "Poor *child*! She's bleeding!"

Hayley was seized and carried away. The pork chop was taken from her like a trophy and she was carried over marshy carpets, first to somebody's bedroom, where Harmony bathed her scraped front and spread soothing ointment there, while cousins ran about finding her some fur slippers and a large fluffy dressing gown. Then, wrapped in these luxuries, she was carried downstairs again. "I can walk!" Hayley protested.

"Yes, but you're not going to – you've saved the day," Aunt May told her.

She ended up in the kitchen, which was still dry and beautifully warm, where the aunts made quarts of cocoa. There Hayley sat in a wooden armchair, surrounded by relatives who were all praising her – except for Tollie, who sat in a corner and glowered at her – sipping cocoa and gradually warming up. Some of the warmth was from the unusual feeling of being the centre of everyone's admiration – apart from Tollie's of course. When Troy appeared, in a red dressing gown, he said, "Well done! You're a brave one, aren't you!" And Aunt May, now wearing a musty-smelling fur coat, hugged her mightily and said, "You courageous child! We won't forget this in a hurry!"

Hayley had never known anything like this.

The warmth from it was still with her when Cousin Mercer carried her up to bed and she fell asleep, into warm, sunny, contented dreams.

Chapter Six

The next day, it was hard to believe that it had ever rained. Hayley woke to find the sky a bright heavenlike blue with great snowy clouds hustling across it. Aunt May woke her by coming in with an armload of clothes.

"Here, dear. Most of these should fit you. Try them on and make sure you're warm enough. The wind's chilly today. Breakfast in half an hour." Aunt May's hair, because it had been soaked last night, was wilder than ever that morning. Half of it fell down as she crossed the room. And she seemed to have found a whole lot of new necklaces. Red amber beads dangled clacking on her shapeless maroon dress when she threw the clothes on Hayley's bed and went dashing away downstairs.

Hayley got up and examined the clothes. There were shorts with pockets, trousers with pockets, jeans, socks, T-shirts, jackets with pockets, sweatshirts with both hoods and pockets, knitted things, but not a single dress or skirt. Hayley could feel her face settling into a beaming smile. She made a careful selection: trousers with pockets, because those were like the ones Troy wore, a T-shirt that said "HEADS I WIN, TAILS YOU LOSE", thick yellow socks, because the trainers were rather big, and a red cardigan, because she suddenly discovered that red was her favourite colour. Feeling baggy and strange and comfortable, she looked in the mirror to do her hair and wondered what Grandma would say. Her hair had gone right out of control in the night. It radiated from her head in curls, tendrils, ringlets and long feathery locks. Hayley had a moment of terrible guilt. She was *never* going to get it neat! Then she thought of Aunt May and realised there was no need to bother here. She dragged a hairbrush through the wildness and went downstairs.

There she was greeted as if she was the most important person in the place. It was almost overwhelming. Aunts jumped up from the big table and bent over her asking anxiously if she was all right and would she like sausages with her bacon and egg or just beans and fried bread. Harmony hurried over with a glass of orange juice for her, and cousins crowded forward with packets of different cereals. "These chocolate ones are *gorgeous!"* one of the girls said. "No, try the nutty kind," someone else persuaded her. "Or would you prefer porridge?" asked Aunt Geta.

"I bet she wouldn't," said Cousin Mercer.

He was right. Grandma had always insisted on porridge. Hayley looked round at the faces leaning eagerly towards her. She gave a beaming smile. "The chocolate ones, please," she said. "And I'd like bacon and egg and sausages and beans *and* fried bread, please."

Tollie was the only person not anxious to look after her. He looked up from a vast bowl of cereal and scowled.

Hayley turned her smile on him. "And fried tomato," she added.

Tollie said, "Greedy pig," and went back to his cereal.

"Yes, but I'm hungry," Hayley said. She was too. She had no trouble at all in packing away the biggest breakfast of her life, with toast and marmalade and tea as well. When it was over she sighed – a comfortable sigh of regret that she could manage no more – and got up with the others to help carry plates and cups back to the kitchen.

Meanwhile, the aunts were discussing what needed to be done to clean up after the flood. Cousin Mercer said he would drive over to the Golf Club and borrow the rollers they used to dry the greens there.

"That'll help with the carpets," Aunt May said, "but we're going to need some of their big blow driers too for the walls and ceilings. You can't repaint those until they're dry, Mercer. And we'll have to polish the floors and the stairs – it's going to take *days*! Harmony, be an angel and keep the children out of the way while we work."

"The game," said the eldest Tigh boy.

Everyone else clamoured, "Yes! The game, the game! You promised!"

"OK, OK!" Harmony said, laughing. "Wellies on, everyone. The paddock's bound to be soaking wet."

There was a rush for the hall and the big cupboard under the stairs, which seemed to contain every possible size of rubber boots – though not many actual pairs. Troy ended up with one red and one blue boot. Someone found Hayley a pink boot with a white flower on it and someone else came up with another that was plain black. Then everyone galloped, in a stampede of different coloured feet, out through the front door and round the house, to a sort of sloping meadow at one side, where they milled around in the wet grass, impatiently waiting for Harmony.

When Harmony appeared – in knee-length green boots that must have been her own – she was carrying a folding card table and a large plastic shopping bag with an eye-splitting swirly design on it. Everyone cheered and crowded up to her while she opened the table and set it up firmly by digging its legs into the slope. Then she put the bag on it and fetched out of it a big bundle of those kind of pointed plastic tags gardeners use to label plants. As she put those down on the table, she said, "OK, let's recap the vow first, since you haven't played for a year. Everyone say after me: I swear not to say a word about what we do in the game to anyone outside this paddock. You say it too, Tollie, and you, Hayley."

Wondering very much about this, Hayley obediently chorused with the rest, "I swear not to say a word about what we do in this game to anyone outside this paddock." Everyone was saying it, quite devoutly, even Tollie.

"Good," Harmony said. "We don't want Uncle Jolyon to know, do we?" Everyone nodded, equally devoutly. "Now I'll go over the rules. First, I put one of these tags into the ground for each of you and that is where you have to start from. It makes a lot of difference where you start, remember? Then I give you each one of these cards." She brought out of the bag a big bundle of cardboard squares held together with a rubber band. There must have been nearly a hundred of them. Some of them were old and tattered and grey, some were quite new. Harmony put the bundle on the table and said, "You stand there and read your card and—" She dug into the bag again and brought out a large clock with Mickey Mouse on the front and put that on the table too. "When the clock starts, you get going and do exactly what it says on your card. And you *have* to get back before it stops or you'll be stuck out there. And—" She fished in the bag again. "The first one back *successfully*, without *cheating*, Tollie, gets this prize." She brought out what was clearly a Christmas tree ornament, made of plastic, in the shape of a golden apple, and put it down with a flourish in the middle of the table. "There."

"Harmony," said the youngest Laxton girl, "I *can* go on my own this year, can't I? I'm quite old now."

"Well, Lucy—" Harmony looked from Lucy to Hayley. "Yes, I suppose you are. You'd make two of Hayley. All right then." While Lucy was dancing about delightedly, making heavy rubbery *flurps* with her boots, Harmony said, "Hayley, I was going to suggest you went with Troy, as this is the first time you've played. Is that all right, Troy?"

Troy nodded in his good-humoured way.

Tollie said, "And *me* – I go alone too."

"You know you always do," Harmony said. "Now—"

"Let's *start*!" Tollie whined. "I'm getting bored."

"Yes," Harmony said. She picked up the bundle of gardener's tags. Hayley saw that each of them had someone's name written on them. There was even one with "HAYLEY" on it. Harmony hurried up and down the paddock with the bundle, digging each one into the ground in a different place and calling out, "Lucy, you're down here. James, up here beside this bush, right? Tollie, off to left here," and so on. Finally, she stuck two tags into the ground together, out to one side. "Troy and Hayley, over here, see?" Then she came back to the table, a bit breathless, and solemnly took the rubber band off the cards. She shuffled the pack, the way you shuffle playing cards. Everyone's eyes fixed on her hands as if this was the most exciting moment of the game. When she started passing the cards out, they were snatched from her and everyone except Troy and Hayley raced away to the markers.

"Harmony," Troy said, lingering. "This is a bit fierce

for someone's first go. Look. Can't you change it?"

Harmony glanced at the card Troy was holding out. It was obvious that she saw what Troy meant, but she shook her head. "Sorry. No. I can't make it work with a change. The only thing you can do is not to play."

"If we *do* play," Troy said, "what sign of the zodiac are we under now?"

Harmony looked up at the sky with its scudding clouds. "Virgo," she said. "Just passed the cusp with Leo. Make up your mind, Troy. Everyone's waiting."

"I suppose Virgo's not so bad," Troy said. "*You* decide," he said, passing the card to Hayley.

The card was old and worn and floppy, and fawn coloured with age. When Hayley took it, she found it had once been a plain postcard on which someone had written – a long time ago, to judge by the way the ink had faded – in large, firm capitals: FETCH A SCALE FROM THE DRAGON THAT CIRCLES THE ZODIAC.

"What do you think?" Troy said to her.

Hayley had no idea what they were supposed to do in the game anyway and the card made her very curious to find out. Besides, everyone else was standing by the markers jigging with impatience. James, who was nearest, said, "Hurry it *up*, can't you!" and Tollie, in the distance, was jumping up and down shouting, "Cowards, cowards, cowards!"

"I think we'd better try," she said.

"Great!" said Troy. He seized her by one arm and towed her over to the double marker. "Leave the card on the grass for Harmony to collect."

Back by the table, Harmony wound up the clock. It seemed to be a musical box as well as a clock. When Harmony set it down on the table, ticking loudly, it began to play a small tinkly tune. Grandpa had played the same tune to Hayley once and told her it was by Mozart.

"*A Little Night Music*?" she said to Troy.

He nodded. "We all hear different tunes," he said. "Harmony's good at that. Start walking."

All over the paddock the others were setting off. James charged downhill towards the orchard. Tollie came rushing back up the hill. Lucy was walking rather carefully in a straight line, looking nervous. Most of the rest were running towards the house.

"Some of them are cheating," Troy said, pulling Hayley forwards. "Tollie always does."

Hayley hastily dropped the card by the markers and let herself be pulled towards the garden shed at the side of the paddock.

It was a simple brick-built shed with a pointed roof, but when they came to it, Hayley was highly delighted to find that the top half of the door was of panes of stained glass, in nine different colours. As Troy pulled the door shut behind them, Hayley saw Lucy pass slowly across outside, from thundery yellow, to stormy red and then to twilight purple as she walked out of sight. Inside, the old lawnmowers and the stack of deckchairs were in a sort of rainbow dusk. Troy, keeping hold of Hayley's wrist, edged them past the lawnmowers – and through some thick, dusty cobwebs that caught unpleasantly on Hayley's hair – and on into coloured twilight beyond. Shortly, it was almost dark. But there seemed to be a passage there, or perhaps even a path, and Troy led her firmly along it.

Path, Hayley decided, as they brushed among leaves and out into some kind of cold dry place. It was very dark here, but Tollie was clearly visible when he rushed suddenly and jeeringly across their way.

"Stupids!" he called out. "You're on the wrong strand!"

Hayley stopped.

"Take no notice," Troy said, pulling at her. "He's always trying to put people off."

"Yes, but where *are* we?" Hayley said.

"Out in the mythosphere by now," Troy answered. "I think we're nearly halfway, but it's bound to get more difficult as we go on."

"Then that's all right," Hayley said. "I've been out here before with Flute. How can you and Tollie do it too?"

"Oh, we can all do it," Troy said. "All our family belongs to the mythosphere, didn't you know?"

"What? Even Grandma?" Hayley exclaimed.

"Of course," Troy said. "But she's one of the ones, like Mercer, who does what Uncle Jolyon says and—"

Here Tollie rushed across their path again, coming the other way. "I'm telling of you!" he shouted, and vanished away into the dark.

Hayley almost stopped again.

"Don't you believe it!" Troy said, hauling her onward. "If he tells tales, he couldn't play. Uncle Jolyon would stop this game like a shot if he knew we were playing it. And," he added, "Harmony would get it in the neck worse than any of us, for inventing it."

Hayley hoped Troy was right. She did not trust Tollie one bit.

They could see the strand they were on now, a silvery, slithery path, coiling away up ahead. The worst part, to Hayley's mind, was the way it didn't seem to be fastened to anything at the sides. Her feet, in their one pink boot and one black, kept slipping. She was quite afraid that she was going to pitch off the edge. It was like trying to climb a strip of tinsel. She hung on hard to Troy's warmer, larger hand and wished it was not so cold. The deep chilliness made the scrapes on the front of her ache.

To take her mind off it, she stared around. The rest of the mythosphere was coming into view overhead and far away, in dim, feathery streaks. Some parts of it were starry swirls, like the Milky Way only white, green and pale pink, and other more distant parts flickered and waved like curtains of light blowing in the wind. Hayley found her chest filling with great admiring breaths at its beauty, and she stared and stared as more and more streaks and strands came into view.

She was taken completely by surprise when a comet came fizzing past her face, with its tail roaring out behind like a rocket. "I'm telling, I'm telling!" it shouted in Tollie's voice. And Hayley went sideways with the shock of it. She had to save herself by clutching the sharp, icy edge of the strand.

Troy hauled her upright. "Oh, go away and play your own game!" he shouted after the comet. "Are you OK, Hayley?"

"Perfectly, thanks." Hayley stood up, shaking her icy hand, and stared scornfully after the comet as it roared away. Grandpa had told her about comets. "He's got it all wrong," she said. "Comets go *tail first*. *Not* like rockets."

Troy laughed as if he couldn't help it. "So much for you, Tollie!" he said. "Come on. We're nearly there."

He was right. They laboured up round another slithery curve, which took them through a copse of silvery trees that rattled as they passed, and then brought them out into black night filled with stars. Everything was made of stars there. Over to the right, a huge lion prowled away from them, shaking a mane that was all stars, pacing on great starry paws and twitching a long tail made of stars. Much nearer to the left, an enormous woman stood still as a statue – except for her hair that was trails of blowing stars – and stared at them with huge, disapproving star eyes.

Unfortunately, Hayley was still remembering the things Grandpa had taught her. "We oughtn't to be able to *breathe* here!" she cried out. "There's no air!" Her lungs heaved in and out, but nothing happened. She knew she was suffocating.

Troy shook her arm. "Don't be silly! This is the mythosphere. I *told* you we both belong to it! Of *course* you can breathe!"

Hayley was rather ashamed to find that he was quite right. As soon as Troy spoke, she stood there breathing in a perfectly normal way. "What do we do now?" she asked, a little sulkily, because she felt stupid.

"Wait for the dragon to arrive, I suppose," Troy said. "I've never been here either."

He looked over to the left, beyond the starry woman, where a huge set of weighing scales was just coming into view. Hayley looked right, towards the lion, hoping it would go on walking away and not notice them. And something swam slowly towards her from beyond the lion. It was a bulky, complicated mass of stars, but as the lion swung its huge head round to look at it, it uncoiled a little and produced a long spiky tail, like a lashing river of stars, and seemed to be warning the lion not to mess with it. The lion lashed its own tail contemptuously and went pacing on, and the dragon floated onwards. It was surrounded in fiery flakes now, like burning snow, that its movements seemed to have dislodged from its tail.

"It's coming," Hayley said, nudging Troy. "It's going the other way."

Troy whirled round, just as the dragon floated level with them. It was coming surprisingly fast, in spite of being all coiled up. It was made of stars fitted together like a mosaic or a jigsaw puzzle and quite blindingly bright. It looked at them as it glided by, out of an eye that was like a small sun deep inside a glass ball.

"Er – hello?" Troy said.

The dragon went on looking and did not answer. But then the huge starry woman noticed it. Slow icy anger came into her remote face and she waved an arm the way a human woman might try to swat a bat. The dragon uncoiled menacingly at her and she snatched her arm back. Next moment the darkness was filled with more burning flakes from the dragon, all blowing towards Troy and Hayley in the wind from the woman's movements. Troy grabbed at one as it sailed past his face and stood holding it while the dragon floated away beyond the huge woman.

"I've got one," he said, looking rather stunned. "We've done it. Come on, let's get back. We might even win."

He took Hayley's hand, and together they went sliding and scrambling down the silvery strip. Sometimes they sat down and slid, sometimes they stood up and ran along the flatter parts, while around them great misty swatches of the mythosphere turned and arched and rippled. Troy hauled Hayley along so fast that she had little time to notice anything they were passing, but she did notice that the star-shaped flake in Troy's other hand grew dimmer as they went. And now that Tollie did not seem to be around to distract her, she caught glimpses of planets whirling in the distance, and saw a centaur – unless it was a man on a horse – and a person who seemed to be half goat, and several odd-looking ladies, and a man with a bull's head. After that she kept glimpsing people, who seemed more like ordinary humans as they went downwards, until Troy dragged her between some bushes and they were once more in the garden shed. By then the thing in Troy's hand was a shiny curved oval that looked like a metal seashell.

Up at the top of the paddock, where Harmony was standing by the table, the clock was still chiming out its tune. Harmony smiled as Troy and Hayley came panting up to her. "Any luck?"

"We got one!" Troy gasped.

"It kept shaking them loose," Hayley explained.

Before Harmony could answer, Lucy came dashing

up, pink and proud and pleased. "I got it! I picked it up when it fell off her foot," she panted, and held out a little glass shoe. "This truly is Cinderella's slipper! Have I won?"

James raced in from one side, equally out of breath, and held out something clenched in his fist. "Prester John's beard is seventy-seven centimetres long and he says we're to stop coming and asking him for hairs all the time." He looked at Lucy, Troy and Hayley. "Damn! Didn't I win? Who did?"

By this time, the clock's little tune was slowing down. Tighs and Laxtons began arriving from all directions. Harmony was soon surrounded by people waving strange objects at her and saying things like "This is Blind Pugh's stick!" or "I got the firebird feather! Look!" or "One Aladdin's lamp, as ordered!"

Harmony picked each object up as it was pushed at her and looked at it very closely. She nodded at the curly grey hair James was holding and at Troy's dragon scale and Lucy's shoe. "Those are genuine," she agreed. "They can go in the trophy cabinet. So can this lamp. Put it down on the table, Charlie, and be careful not to rub it.

But you got this feather from the vase in the lounge, didn't you, Sarah? Go and put it back. Yes, this says DRINK ME – it's from *Alice* all right. But this isn't a walking stick, Oliver. It looks like a broom handle to me."

"But I was in the inn when Blind Pugh arrived!" Oliver protested.

"Then he must have fooled you," Harmony replied. "He may be blind, but he *is* a pirate, you know. Yes, the drinking horn truly was used by Beowulf. That can go in the cabinet and so can this One Ring. No, don't put it *on*, you fool! It's dangerous!"

All this time, the tune from the clock was going slower and slower. Just as the last three notes were dragging out, Tollie came staggering up, looking exhausted but pleased with himself. "Here you are," he said. "Bowl of porridge from the Three Bears!" and he dumped it on the table.

Harmony looked at it and sighed. "That's from the kitchen here," she said. "Why must you always cheat, Tollie?"

"Because he wastes his time rushing about the strands trying to put the rest of us off!" James said.

"I don't think he should be allowed to play."

"Hear, hear!" said almost everybody else. "He's a pest!"

"We'll see," Harmony said soothingly. "Everyone come indoors to the cabinet for the presentation."

As they all trooped towards the house, where Sarah joined them, looking decidedly ashamed of herself, Hayley whispered to Troy, "Why did she let Tollie get away with it?"

Troy made a face. "Because he's quite capable of telling his dad - Mercer, you know - and Mercer would tell Uncle Jolyon at once. It's blackmail really."

The trophy cabinet was in a small room off the lounge. Although the lounge was now dry and polished, nobody had yet got round to the small room. On its wet and muddy floor stood a tall glass-fronted cupboard which Harmony unlocked with a special key from the plastic bag. Inside, on the rather dirty shelves, were little heaps of tiny objects: quite a pile of inch long glass shoes, almost a nest of grey curly hairs, six miniature Aladdin's lamps, a bunch of tiny bright feathers and a cluster of little bottles, among other things. Harmony ceremoniously put the new objects beside the old, small ones, where they sat dwarfing them. Last of all, she put Troy's big gleaming dragon scale beside the three tiny ones already there. Then she locked the cupboard and turned to give the plastic apple into Hayley's hands.

"There," she said. "I'm giving the prize to Hayley because she was pretty brave to go. Is that OK, Troy?"

"Fine," Troy said, in his calm way. "I've won a hundred times anyway."

Chapter Seven

For the next few days, Hayley enjoyed herself more than she had ever done in her entire life. Once the aunts had finished drying and cleaning the house and Mercer was able to set up ladders and start the repainting, Troy explained the rules of hide-and-seek and the other indoor games. Hayley rushed shrieking through the rooms and corridors with her cousins as if she had been doing it all her life. She ate huge meals. She went with the rest of them in a convoy of cars to the seaside, where the sea took her breath away, first by its size and strength, and again when Troy and Harmony tried to teach her to swim and an enormous wave rolled in and swamped all three of them.

"Getting quite rosy and plump, isn't she?" beautiful Aunt Alice said to Aunt May as the two of them lay stretched on towels, watching. And Aunt May agreed, rather proudly, feeling personally responsible for the change in Hayley.

Apart from that one day by the sea, the young ones played the game most mornings and Hayley soon began to feel a veteran of the mythosphere. Harmony always insisted that Hayley went with Troy for safety, but Hayley did not mind, even when Tollie chanted, "Baby, baby! Has to have her hand held!"

"Take no notice," Harmony said. "He's a brat."

"I know," said Hayley. "Harmony, why do you always manage the game? Don't you ever want to play too?"

A thoughtful, amused look came over Harmony's face. "Well," she said, "for one thing, I'm the only one who *can* manage it. And for another, when I was small, I used to ramble all over the mythosphere, until my mother caught me at it and threatened to tell Uncle Jolyon."

"Daren't you go now?" Hayley asked anxiously, thinking of how angry Grandma had been.

Harmony laughed. "Don't worry. I still go out there a lot – but mostly when I'm away at Music College, so that I won't get Mother into trouble." She took up the bundle of markers and looked around the paddock, where everyone was waiting to start that morning's game. "Where's Troy got to?"

Troy came into the paddock as Harmony asked this. He said to Harmony, "Mercer's going to finish the painting today."

Hayley was surprised. She had grown so used to seeing Cousin Mercer up a ladder painting water-stained ceilings that it almost seemed like his permanent occupation – and from the number of ceilings needing painting, anyone would have thought Cousin Mercer would be up a ladder at least for the next year.

Harmony looked musingly down at the card table, with the clock and the bundle of cards on it. "I think we'd better make this the last game then," she said.

Everybody groaned.

Harmony simply fixed Tollie with a meaning stare. "Isn't that so, Tollie?"

Tollie shuffled his trainers in the trampled grass. "I told him all about the game. He's going to phone Uncle Jolyon as soon as he's finished," he admitted.

"You little sneak," Harmony said to him, in a dangerously kind, cheerful voice. "I hope you realise you've spoilt your own fun too."

Tollie pointed at Hayley. "It's *her* fault. She shouldn't be playing."

Harmony tossed her hair back angrily. "*None* of us should be playing," she said. "Don't you understand, you silly little brat? No, you don't, do you? Right everyone. As this is our last game, we'll add a bit of variety. Each of you take your own marker and plant it where you like. That should change the strands you use quite radically. Then come back and get your card." She spread the markers out in a fan on the table and then picked up the cards and shuffled them, still staring at Tollie. "If I didn't know you'd cheat," she said, as Hayley picked up her marker and went off beside Troy to plant it, "I'd make sure you got the

Slough of Despond or the cave of Polyphemus, Tollie. Polyphemus is a man-eating giant and just what you deserve."

Tollie gave Harmony a smirk. He planted his marker right beside the card table and held out his hand for a card. Harmony handed it to him with a sugary smile. "There you are, dear Tollie. Fetch a roc's egg and I hope it chokes you. And I warn you – if you bring me the ostrich egg from Aunt May's office, I shall break all my promises to Mercer and spank you."

She handed cards out to everyone else. From the looks on all their faces, the instructions on the cards were not the usual ones. Lucy went quite white as she read hers. "I'm *afraid* of witches!" she whispered to James.

"Bad luck," James said unsympathetically. "You're lucky – *I've* got to get through a dirty great thorn hedge, and I don't even know what a spindle *looks* like! What happens if I wake Sleeping Beauty up?" he asked Harmony.

She handed a card to Hayley. "Why, you get married and live happily ever after, James my sweetheart," she said. "Look on the bright side. You'd be safe away from Uncle Jolyon if that happens."

It was evident that Harmony was very angry indeed. As they went back to their markers, Troy said nervously to Hayley, "What does she want *us* to do?"

Hayley looked at her card. It said, FETCH A GOLDEN APPLE FROM THE ORCHARD OF THE HESPERIDES. Though it was as used and battered looking as any of the other cards, when she showed it to Troy, he said, "I've never seen *that* one before! But it doesn't look too bad. Last time she got this angry, I had to go to Mercury and bring her a mad robot. And the time before that, I had to pinch Arthur's sword out of the stone. I couldn't pull it out and he came along and hit me for trying to steal it. And before that— Oh, forget it. Let's go."

Behind them, the clock started to tinkle. This time its tune was *Over the Rainbow*, which made Hayley laugh, because it seemed exactly right. She followed Troy down to the bottom of the paddock, where there was a small gate that led into the orchard. That struck her as exactly right too.

The next moment she was wondering if it *was* right.

Troy pushed the gate open and walked in among all the bushy apple trees. Hayley followed him before the gate swung closed again, but there was no sign of Troy when she was in the orchard. Since there was a clear path trodden through the long grass, Hayley followed it, expecting all the time to see Troy ahead of her beyond the next tree. Instead, she came to another fence with a gate in it, that led out into a wide field. She could not see Troy anywhere in the field. But in the distance there was a man driving a tractor – or maybe a digger – up a steep slope. Hayley set out towards him to ask if he had seen Troy go past.

There seemed to be something wrong with the digger – or tractor. It would get some way up the hill and then its engine would stop and the machine would go sliding backwards downhill. Hayley could see the man bobbing about, trying to put on the brake and start the engine again. Before long, she could hear him swearing. But before she got near enough to hear actual swearwords, Tollie came racing up and stopped in front of her.

"You're going *wrong*!" he cried out. "You can't go this way!"

He sounded as if he was desperate for her to believe him. But Hayley, like Harmony, felt she had had enough of Tollie. "Oh, go *away*!" she said. "Go and find your roc's egg and stop trying to cheat!" She pushed past Tollie and marched on across the field.

She could hear Tollie shouting behind her, but by then, in the strange way of the mythosphere, the hill and the stalled digger were not there any more. Hayley found herself instead stumbling among loose rocks in some kind of mountain pass. The pass very shortly opened out into a stony valley, bare and barren except for small yellowing bushes that smelt like turkey stuffing. There were steep mountains on either side and not a sign of Troy anywhere.

Hayley faltered. Tollie must have been right and she really had gone the wrong way. But then she thought how Tollie was always trying to put people off and marched on, sliding and stumbling among the stones.

There was a particularly huge mountain over to her left, very strangely shaped. The top of it was covered in grey, smoky, shifting clouds, but the lower part – the part she could see – looked almost like a pair of great stone feet, with a sort of hump beyond that. This hump, for some reason, made Hayley very uneasy. She kept her eyes on it as she hurried and stumbled through the valley. At first it was simply an odd-shaped crag, with clouds streaming across it, dimming it, veiling it, and then showing it again, but it changed shape as Hayley moved on. By the time she came level with it, it was looking remarkably like an enormous stone woman, crouching on the mountainside and peering out at the valley. Hayley was just below it when the clouds suddenly smoked away from the rocky nose, for a moment unveiling piercing eyes and a stern mouth. Hayley almost screamed. It looked exactly like Grandma's face made of stone.

"Oh, heavens!" Hayley said. "No, no, *no*!"

She put her hands to the sides of her face and ran. Her feet clattered and slipped on stones and then shortly slapped on water. She was among trees after that, where her hair caught painfully on twigs. She crouched over and went on running, terrified that great stone feet were coming tramping after her, to tell her she was forbidden to be here and *certainly* not with her hair all loose and wearing a loud red cardigan. Her panic took her through snow next and then through rain, and after that along a windy seashore where her trainers filled with sand and slowed her almost to a walk. But she did not stop trying to run until she came into a green place full of sunshine. People were playing music there.

The music made Hayley feel safe – very safe, because it was one of the tunes Fiddle used to play beside the pub, on the shady side of the street. Hayley sat down on the grass, half hidden by a tree, to empty the sand out of her shoes and get her breath back, and stared out into the glade with great interest. There was a bit of a feast going on out there. There was a table made of logs, with wineglasses and bread and fruit on it and a large leather pitcher to hold the wine. Three very pretty ladies in floaty dresses were sitting along a garden seat beyond the table, entertaining an old man and two more ladies who had their backs to Hayley. One musical lady played the flute, the one in the middle had a sort of banjo, and the third one kept the beat with a sort of tinkly rattle. When they finished the tune, the three people at the table clapped and raised their wineglasses. The musical ladies laughed. The one playing the flute said, "I think we have a visitor, Papa." And she pointed at Hayley with her flute.

The old man whirled round in his seat. "Who?" he said.

To Hayley's astonishment, he was Grandpa – Grandpa wearing a loose grey-blue robe, but Grandpa all the same, and looking much more cheerful than he usually did at home on the edge of London. He stared at Hayley and burst out laughing.

"Well, I'll be – *Hayley*!" he said. "I hardly knew you in those clothes! Come over here and be introduced to your aunts." And, again most unlike his usual self, he held out both arms to her.

Hayley slowly stood up. "Is Grandma here?" she asked cagily.

Grandpa shook his head. "No, no, she never comes here. It's much too free and easy for her – and much too full of strange things."

He continued to hold out his arms to her, so Hayley

went over to him and let herself be folded into a hearty hug.

"Merope's daughter," Grandpa explained to the ladies across her head.

"Oh, I remember!" said the lady Hayley could see out of her left eye. She wore a gown the blue of hyacinths and she had two deep dimples when she smiled. "Merope got into trouble for marrying a mortal, didn't she?"

"And so did the mortal, poor fellow," Grandpa said. He swung Hayley round into the crook of his left arm. "This one in blue," he told her, "is your aunt Arethusa, and the one in green is your aunt Hespere. That one with the flute is Aigley and the one with the sistrum is Hesperethusa. Erytheia is our string player. If you want to talk about them all together, you call them the Hesperides."

Hayley looked from one to the other of these five pretty ladies. There was a strong family likeness between them all, although Arethusa was fair and rounded and Erytheia thin and dark, with the others in between in various ways. They were each wearing a different coloured gown and all smiled at Hayley as if they were delighted to meet her. So many aunts! Hayley thought. Oh, I understand! This is Grandpa's other family that he goes to see. "Now I've got *nine* aunts!" she said wonderingly.

"Well, actually you've got eleven really," Grandpa said. "There are seven of the Pleiades, you know. There must be two you haven't met yet."

"Oh, yes. There's Harmony and Troy's mother," Hayley remembered. "None of them is as beautiful as you," she said to the five new aunts.

They laughed, and laughed again when Grandad protested, "Oh, I don't know! Alcyone is quite a looker, don't you think? Even Maia could be if she tried. And Asterope would be prettiest of all if she wasn't such a mouse. I love and admire all my daughters, Hayley." Then he turned a little stern and asked, "Now what are you doing here? Did you just wander along, or did you come for a reason?"

"We were wondering that too," said Hespere, the one in green.

"For a reason," Hayley said. "For Harmony's game. I

have to bring back a golden apple from the Garden of the Hesperides. That's from you, isn't it?"

The new aunts looked at one another and then at Grandpa, anxiously. "That's not as easy as you'd think," said Arethusa, the one in blue. "We'd give you an apple, gladly, if it was only up to us."

Aigley, the flute player, who wore a dress like a daffodil, explained, "The apple trees are very well guarded, you see, by a dragon called Ladon."

"And they all belong to the king," Erytheia said, propping her banjo-like instrument against the garden seat, "who knows exactly how many apples there are."

"You, Grandpa?" Hayley asked hopefully. "Are you king here?"

Grandpa shook his head. "Not me, my love. I'm only a Titan. I'm not that grand."

Erytheia stood up and straightened her white dress. "I'll take her to the gate and show her," she said. "I can advise her at least."

"I'll come too," Hesperethusa said, laying down her rattle.

"Good. Bless you both," Grandpa said. "Tell her what

to do. And come back in one piece, Hayley, even if you have to do it without an apple." He gave her another hug and pushed her towards her two aunts.

Feeling very nervous now, Hayley set off with Erytheia rippling along in her white dress on one side and Hesperethusa floating gracefully on the other. Hesperethusa's dress was a lovely blushing pink, like the best kind of sunset. Hayley was sure that, if her aunts had not been there, she would have run away and cheated like Tollie, probably by bringing Harmony the plastic apple she had won on the first day.

But they were there, and they led her among the trees to a tall fence with a tall gate in it. Through its bars there wafted the most intense fragrance of apples – not the dull, cidery scent apples have when they have been picked, but that fresh, living smell apples have when they are ripe but still growing on the tree.

"Now listen, love," Erytheia said, with her hand on the latch of the gate, "if anything goes wrong, or even *starts* to go wrong, go at *once* to the very end of this strand of the mythosphere."

"Everything hardens off there and turns into stars," Hesperethusa added. "You'll probably be a star of some sort yourself out there, but don't be afraid. Nothing much can hurt our family out at the edge there. Just alter your path a little and go home another way."

"All right," Hayley said. Her voice had gone down to a whisper.

Both ladies bent and kissed her. Feeling so nervous that the skin of her stomach tightened and jumped under the nearly healed scratches from her first night in Ireland, Hayley slipped round the gate and in amongst the apple trees. Apples hung all about her, just above the level of her head. They did not look brightly gold. They were more like ordinary apples, with their gold fuzzed over with brown and some red streaks amid the brown. But they were obviously gold, for all that, drooping heavy on the tree, just as they were obviously growing and alive.

This looks too easy! Hayley thought suspiciously. But she stretched up her hand to pick the nearest apple.

"Er – *hem*!" said the dragon Ladon.

He was coiled round the trunk of that tree. His

scales were the same crusty grey as the lichen on the trunk of the tree, which was why Hayley had not seen him up to then.

Chapter Eight

Hayley froze, with her arm up and her fingers curled round ready to pick the apple, and simply did not dare to move. She hardly dared breathe. She was too scared even to think.

"What do you think you're doing?" the dragon said. His steamy breath wafted round Hayley as he spoke. It smelt like a wood fire, sooty and woody at once.

Hayley thought she had lost her voice. It took a real effort to whisper, "Please, sir, I need a golden apple."

"You can't have one," said the dragon. "Do you think I'm going to let you loose in the mythosphere with something that precious?" He rolled an eye at her, while his breath coiled up among the leaves of the tree, filling it with fog. Hayley stared at his eye. It was like looking into a far distant sun deep inside a glass ball. "Don't I know you?" the dragon said, filling the tree with fog again. "A tasty morsel – lots of hair and a body that's half red? " His long face left the tree trunk and began to stretch out towards Hayley. "Didn't you come with a friend and steal one of my old scales the other day?" The tip of his nose was nearly on Hayley's chest by then.

He's going to *eat* me! Hayley thought.

The realisation unfroze her mind and she remembered Erytheia's advice. "Yes, I was there," she said. She managed to bend her stiff body and jacknife herself away to the outer edge of the mythosphere.

Everywhere was stars suddenly.

At least that meant that the dragon was quite a long way off. Hayley could see his starry jigsaw puzzle shape drifting in the distance, just beyond the huge starry woman, who seemed to have turned herself round to watch him as he glided towards the mighty weighing scales. Beyond the weighing scales, an enormous starry insect with an arched up tail was just coming into view. When Hayley looked the other way, she could see the lion, and a crab receding into the distance beyond the lion.

I suppose it's better to be safe and not have an apple, she thought sadly.

Something rustled tinnily above and beside her.

Hayley was sure the dragon had somehow crept up behind her. She froze again. But when she managed to make herself turn slowly round towards the noise, she discovered it was made by starry leaves rattling on a silver tree. It was the wood where she had come with Troy. She was still in an orchard of sorts, except that this one was made of stars. Trees stood all around her, gently quivering in the solar wind, each one heavy with round, moony fruit. Some of the fruits were blue, some silver-white, and some gently shining a faint, peachy gold.

"Heaventrees!" Hayley whispered, and wondered who had told her or where she had read of the trees of heaven.

It doesn't matter, she thought. Moving very slowly

and gently, she carefully chose the nearest, most golden looking of the fruit and crept her hand out towards it. As soon as her fingers were around it, she plucked it off its starry twig. It went *twing.*

The head of the distant dragon whipped round towards her in a cloud of fiery flakes, but by then it was too late. Hayley clutched the golden apple in both hands and became a comet.

She was a proper comet, not like Tollie's pretend one. Her hair gathered together and flung itself out ahead of her like the flame on a blowtorch. Behind it, her body was a small, curled-up, icy ball. But because she was clutching the golden apple, she knew she was carrying with her all the seeds of life – all excitement, joy, growth and adventure. She could go anywhere in the universe with this and still be alive.

She forged off on her strange, eccentric comet's path. She felt as if she was going crazily fast, bombing along – and yet, at the same time, it felt like a slow, stately progress. She wheeled away from the zodiac and that fell slowly behind, the woman, the lion, the crab, and two starry men who seemed to be twins, all swinging aside and away like the view from a train window when the train is going really fast. And as soon as the zodiac was out of sight, Hayley discovered that being a comet was more fun than she had ever had in her life. She zoomed along, laughing.

Her comet course, she knew, was a long thin oval. Since she was outward bound at the moment, in order to get back to Earth, she knew she was going to have to rush out to her very limit and then turn a hairpin bend before she could head back sunwards. That meant at least a light year of rushing. "Whoopee!" she shrieked as she sped outwards.

It was bliss. It went on for ages. But at last she felt her speed dropping, as if she was coming near the end of her orbit. Turn the corner, she thought. *Now!*

She swooped herself sideways. If she had had wheels, they would have squealed and smoked with her speed. Hayley shrieked again at the joy and danger of it. And, as she careered madly right, and right, and right again, she remembered Hesperethusa's advice, to alter her path and go home a different way. Or that dragon will be waiting, she thought. So, when she came to the last bit of her turn, she swooped herself just a little bit more to the right and went rushing off again not quite the way she had come.

And it was still bliss. Stars streaked past, pale, bright, red, blue and greenish yellow, forming themselves into starry animals, birds and people as they whirled by. Hayley bombed happily onwards, until one set of stars turned itself slowly into an enormous bear. The Great Bear, she thought, and knew she was almost home.

Sure enough, if she peered forward and down through the veils of her own hair, she could see the Solar System looking just like it did on Grandpa's computer. There was the sun in the middle and all the planets sedately circling it. She saw big Neptune and heavy, white Uranus, ringed Saturn and Jupiter looking sultry and yellow, with red blotches on it. Pluto was lurking somewhere out in the dark, while little Mercury and cloudy Venus seemed much too near the sun and likely to fry in its heat. And there circled red Mars and blue Earth.

Hayley began to hope she was aimed properly at

Earth, but as she hurtled onwards, it began to look much more as if she was heading straight for the sun. Comets did sometimes plunge into the sun, she knew. Grandpa had told her. She tried to sidle herself more into a line for Earth, but she couldn't. The sun was actually *pulling* her.

"Oh, help!" she said. "I'm going to *die*. What a waste, now I've discovered I can do *this*!"

Then, before she had totally panicked, it seemed as if she was only going to pass very near the sun – to slide by perhaps a mere million miles away. She could already feel the blazing heat from it. When she looked at it, she could clearly see the twirling sunspots and the hissing, leaping lumps of flame. And she could see the person in green clothes standing in the hard, hot midst of it.

"*What*?" Hayley thought. "People *can't*—"

She was still only halfway through that thought, when the person in the sun waved at her and shouted. "*Stop*!" he yelled. "Match velocities *now*!"

Hayley found herself – not exactly slowing – gliding beside the sun at about the same speed and much too near for comfort. The heat of it uncurled her, melting her from around her apple. "Don't *do* that!" she shouted. And found herself looking across at Flute. "Oh, of course," she said. "Fiddle said you stood in the sun."

Flute stood with his arms folded, surrounded in leaping hissing heat. He did not look entirely friendly. "Until this morning," he said, "I had a thousand and one golden apples. Now I've only got a thousand."

"Are they *yours*?" Hayley said. "I didn't know—"

Flute nodded, his hair leaping among the white hot flames. "And you've got another one in your pocket," he said.

Up until then, Hayley had clean forgotten that she had zipped Harmony's prize apple into one of her trouser pockets. She would have liked to pat that pocket to make sure the plastic apple there was still safe, but she was a little too icy and curled up to do that. She said airily, "Oh, that's only a plastic apple Harmony gave me for a prize in the game."

Flute grinned a little. "*Is* it? That girl Harmony has stolen more of my apples than I care to think of. She now has the run of the universe, probably the whole *multiverse*. She's *everywhere*, in spite of your uncle Jolyon's orders. Don't go giving her that new one."

"I won't then," Hayley said. "I want to keep it."

Flute lost his grin. "Do you? Then you realise you'll have to pay me for it, don't you? My apples are never free."

"Oh," said Hayley. It was a relief, in a way, to know that she need not be a thief. She hated the idea that she had been stealing from Flute of all people. But it had never occurred to Grandma to give Hayley any money before sending her away. Glumly, knowing she was penniless, Hayley asked, "How much do you want for it?"

"I'll take," said Flute, "one of the stars from Orion's bow. We want that quite urgently, as it happens."

"Er—" Hayley began.

"I know you haven't got it now," said Flute. "You can give it me when you next see me. And I want your promise that you will."

"I promise," Hayley said, feeling small and sad. She thought, I'll have to ask Harmony what I do about that. Oh, *dear*.

"Very well," said Flute. "Off you go then."

Hayley peered through the cloudy spout of her hair

and tried to turn herself towards Earth, which had moved quite a way further in its orbit while they talked. She would never have managed it, if Flute had not reached out and given her a shove. This sent her gliding off on a course that would meet Earth as it went on round.

"See you soon," he called as Hayley headed away.

She was still moving quite fast, but to her disappointment not hurtling along any more. She was simply travelling on her own inertia and getting cooler again as she moved. She went from hot, to warm, to balmy, to lukewarm and, in spite of this, she melted steadily. Even when she glided into truly cold air somewhere on the night side of Earth, she was still melting. Dripping and distressed, she came uncurled in darkness and her hair fell back again around her shoulders as she landed and knew she was a human girl again. It was a dreadful loss. Hayley could not help sobbing a little as she stood still and carefully stowed the golden apple in another pocket with a zip. She sniffed and wondered which way to go.

Someone came up to her in the near dark and said, "You need to take this strand here."

Hayley peered. She could see the strand, if she strained, like a path made of coal. "It doesn't look very inviting," she said.

"Well, you *are* on the dark side here," the man said.

Hayley was sure she recognised his voice. She turned and peered up at his face. Under a black cap, his hair seemed white, and it blew about rather. "You're Fiddle!" she said. "I've just met your brother again. And," she added miserably, "I'm not a comet any more."

"I know," Fiddle said. "You can always be one again later."

Hayley's eyes seemed to have got keener for her time as a comet. She could pick out Fiddle's face quite clearly now. Although it was a sad face, it really was remarkably like Flute's. "Are you and Flute twins, by any chance?" she asked him.

"That's right," he said. "We take it in turns to stand in the sun."

Chapter Nine

Fiddle came a little way along the coaly path with Hayley. He said he wanted to make sure she didn't miss the way, but Hayley was fairly sure he was being kinder than that. There seemed to be horrible things going on on either side of the path. There were screams and groans, and somewhere someone who sounded to be dying kept saying, "Water! *Water*! Oh, please, *water!*" Fiddle hurried Hayley along and Hayley tried not to look, until they came to a place where the air was full of desperate panting and a sort of grinding sound. Hayley could not help looking here.

There was a hill to one side and she could dimly see someone trying to heave a boulder up it. All she could really see was a pair of straining legs in ragged trousers, some way above her head. But just as she looked, the person lost control of the boulder and it came rolling and crashing down, bringing the man with it. "Oh, *curses*!" he cried out, ending up in a heap, half under the boulder, almost at Hayley's feet.

"Is he all right?" Hayley said to Fiddle. She thought the man might be crying.

Fiddle pushed her on. "Not really," he said. "But there are no bones broken. He has to get up and push the stone again until he gets it to the top of the hill."

"*Why*?" said Hayley.

"Because your uncle Jolyon says so," Fiddle said. "He's in charge here. This is what happens to people who offend him."

Hayley was glad to think she had never liked Uncle Jolyon. "Can't anyone *stop* him?" she said.

"Not very easily," Fiddle said, "though they tell me that a seer called the Pythoness said it could be done. We're trying to find a way. Now this is where I have to leave you. You'll find things become more and more normal from here on, but do try to keep going whatever you see."

"Will I see you again?" Hayley said.

"Quite probably," Fiddle answered. He waved to her and turned back up the path.

Hayley sadly watched him go. Even though she had only talked to him once and nodded to him with Martya, she always thought of Fiddle as her first real friend. She sighed and walked on.

The path became a passage with barred prison cells on either side of it. Behind one of the thick doors, someone was yelling out, "I hate the lot of you! The whole *lot* of you!" From behind other doors, chains clinked.

I suppose this is more normal, Hayley thought, shivering.

She marched on. The passage went from arched stone to dingy brick and then to modern-looking concrete with strip lights in the ceiling, but there were still prison cells on either side. She came to a squarer part, where soldiers with guns were kicking someone who was writhing about on the floor. This *was* more normal, Hayley supposed. There had been scenes like this on Grandpa's telly. But seen up close it was very nasty.

"You ought to be ashamed of yourselves!" she told the soldiers.

Only one of them took any notice. He swivelled his gun round to point at Hayley. "Get out!" he said to her. And the woman soldier who seemed to be in charge snapped, "Shoot her," without looking up from kicking.

Hayley moved on in a hurry. There seemed to be nothing else she could do. Next moment, she was in a huge office, very brightly lighted, where people sat at desks in rows, all hard at work with computers and telephones. Hayley pattered quickly down the space at the side of the desks, hoping not to be noticed, until she came to the desk at the very end, where there was a man who seemed to be working harder than all the others put together.

Here something made Hayley stop and look. This man had a large tray marked IN on one side of his desk, piled with papers, forms and plastic files. He was snatching these out at the rate of two a minute, studying them swiftly, marking some with a pen, putting some in a copier and then snatching them out, making notes about them on his computer, signing both copies and slapping them into a smaller tray marked OUT. Then he snatched up another set. He was going so quickly that Hayley was sure that he was going to get the IN-tray empty any second. But, just as he was down to one file and two forms, someone came along and dumped another huge pile on top of them. The man groaned and started working on those.

What had made Hayley stop and stare, however, was not how hard the man was working: it was the look of him. He had black curly hair and a brownish skin. The curly hair was receding from his wrinkled forehead and there were rays of further wrinkles fanning from the sides of his big black eyes. He looked familiar. The way he moved was a way Hayley knew. In fact, although he was not young, he looked extraordinarily like the young man in the wedding photo that Grandma kept on Hayley's mantelpiece.

"Excuse me," she said to him. The man looked up.

The moment he did, Hayley was absolutely sure who he was. "What's your name?" she asked him.

"Foss," he said. "Cyrus Foss. Forgive me – I've got so much work—"

"Then you're my dad!" Hayley said. "I'm Hayley Foss."

The man had bent over his papers again, but now he put them down and stared. "Hayley?" he said. "We had a baby girl called Hayley."

"That's me!" Hayley said delightedly. They stared at one another wonderingly. "Why are you here?" Hayley asked.

"Being punished," her father said glumly, "for marrying Merope. It was forbidden. I never understood why, but I knew there was some kind of prophecy. So you're Hayley? You don't look much like your mother, but you've grown up very pretty. Where have you been all this time? Were you being punished too?"

"I'm all right," Hayley assured him. "I had to live with Grandpa. He's all right, but Grandma *isn't*. Can't you leave here now, so that I can live with *you*?"

"No," said her father sadly. "I've tried to leave over

and over, but I always find myself back at this desk, whatever I do."

"But it looks *awful*!" Hayley said.

"It is," he said. "You know what it feels like? It feels as if I'm rolling a huge stone up a hill, and every time I get it nearly to the top, it rolls straight down to the bottom again."

Hayley thought of the man she had seen crashing down the hill under the boulder. That had been her father too. This was the way the mythosphere worked. Things got harsher and stranger the further out you were in it. "Oh!" she cried out. "Isn't there *any* way I can rescue you from here?"

Cyrus Foss smiled at her. It was a harrassed smile, but Hayley had seldom seen a nicer one. "I don't think you can," he said. "But maybe your mother could."

"So where is she?" Hayley demanded.

"Somewhere else in this hell," he said. "She—"

He was interrupted by an office lady carrying a neat pile of shiny plastic files. "These are all wrong," this lady said. ""They all have to be done again." She dumped the files on top of the stack already in the IN-tray. The stack was too high to take them. Every one of them slithered off sideways and fell on the floor, taking half the rest of the papers with them.

Cyrus Foss gave a moan of despair and bent down to collect them. Hayley dived down under the desk to help. Face to face down there, her father whispered, "She'll be in a women's strand, somewhere much wilder than here, I think."

"Right," Hayley whispered back. She crawled across under the desk and stuck her head out beside the office lady's neat feet. "Can't you help?" she said.

"Not my job," the lady said coldly.

"But *you* made them fall down," Hayley pointed out.

"I don't want to ladder my tights," the lady retorted. "And you shouldn't be here. You're interrupting this prisoner in his work. You'd better leave here before the manager finds you."

"Cow!" Hayley's father murmured, with his face still under the desk. He added loudly, "Yes, better leave Hayley. We don't want you in trouble too."

"All right," Hayley said. "See you." She scrambled violently out past the lady's neat feet, hoping she would ladder the tights as she went, and stood up among the other desks. "I'll be back," she told the lady. "So watch out." But the lady simply turned and walked away.

Hayley threaded her way between the busy desks and came to a door. She turned round there to wave to her father, but he was frantically at work again and did not look up. Hayley sighed – the kind of sigh you seem to drag up from near your knees – and pushed her way out through the door.

Outside, the strand leading away in front of her was cloudily transparent now, like smoked glass. Hayley hurried along it, blinking back tears and refusing to look at any of the dreary scenes happening on either side of her, until the strand suddenly turned almost as clear as air underneath her feet. She found herself walking high above the jumbled roofs and turrets of Aunt May's guesthouse. She could see the gutter and the window she had squeezed out of the day she arrived. Ahead of her and below her were the grounds of the place, full of racing figures as the Tighs and the Laxtons all hurried towards the paddock, where Harmony was standing by the card table. Hayley could hear the clock, chiming out *Over the Rainbow*, but very slowly, as if it had almost run down. And Tollie had almost won. He was halfway up the paddock, pushing and rolling an immense egg. This reminded Hayley so of the man pushing the boulder that she stood still and shuddered.

Then, Hey! she thought. I can *win*!

She ran. She came charging down the almost unseeable glassy strand, brushed past Tollie and his egg and landed panting in front of the card table. Tollie screamed with fury.

"That does it!" he yelled. "I'm telling!"

"I've got one – a golden apple!" Hayley panted to Harmony.

Harmony seemed to have got over her bad temper. She smiled and said, "Let's see it then."

Hayley unzipped her pocket and fetched the apple out. For a moment it glowed bright as a small sun and smelled wonderfully of apple. But as Hayley held it out towards Harmony, it was a plastic Christmas ornament just like the ones Harmony gave out as prizes. "Oh!" Hayley said. "But it *was*! It really *is*!"

"I know," Harmony said. "They go like that here." And she passed Hayley another apple just the same. "Your prize," she said.

"I hate you both!" Tollie snarled, leaning both arms on his vast egg. "Still" he added smugly, "I stole a lot of diamonds too. And I'm still telling of Hayley."

James arrived then, waving what looked like a spike with threads of silk streaming off one end. "Is this it?" he asked Harmony. "It was on her spinning wheel. But it was a real closie. She sort of half woke up and said 'Kiss me!' and I just *ran*!"

Lucy pushed up from the other side with a dry-looking slice of cake in one hand. "Out of her cottage wall," she panted. "She saw me and she chased me all the way back here. I don't think I want to play this game again."

"*I've* got a roc's egg!" Tollie said loudly.

He went on saying this as the others began arriving, waving peculiar objects and jostling Hayley about as she carefully zipped both apples into her pockets. "Do these look like thumbscrews?" she heard someone ask.

"I know it looks like a handful of jelly," said someone else, "but it really *is* an eyeball."

"*I've* got a roc's egg!"

"This card really *was* the Queen of Hearts, honestly. It's alive. It sort of squiggles."

"I caught the fox, but he bit me and got away. Do I need an injection, Harmony?"

"*I've* got a roc's egg!"

"Sorry about the blood, Harmony. He'd just killed her when I got there. It was horrible."

"*I've* got a roc's egg!"

"Oh, be quiet, Tollie!" Harmony snapped. "What's the matter, Troy?"

"*And* I'm telling," Tollie mumbled, as Troy arrived last of all, very quiet and dejected.

"I couldn't find that garden anywhere," Troy said. "So I came back and the strand took me through the house for some reason. Mercer's on the phone in the hall. He's telling Uncle Jolyon all about the game."

"Isn't that all we need!" Harmony said. She scooped the cards, the markers and the clock into her coloured bag and snapped the table together. "Everyone go and put their stuff in the trophy cabinet. It'll be open for you. Tollie, you'll have to leave that egg there and hope Uncle Jolyon doesn't notice it. Troy, Hayley, come with me. We'd better find Aunt May."

Aunt May was hurrying out of the house as they came to it. She let Tollie, followed by the crowd of Tighs and Laxtons, rush indoors past her and stopped Harmony, Troy and Hayley.

"Quick," she said. "Jolyon's on his way here already. I wish Mercer wasn't so damn dutiful, but Jolyon *is* his father, you know. Jolyon had no idea that Hayley was here with us, and he's furious. We've got to get her away."

"Does he know about the game?" Harmony asked.

"No – if he knew she'd been playing *that*, he'd go berserk!" Aunt May said distractedly. "But I'd get her away even if she hadn't been. Hayley, you're a darling and you saved us from the flood and what's been done to you is a *shame*. Harmony, Troy, think what to do, *quickly.*"

"We were supposed to be taking her to Mum when we left," Troy said. "To go to school in Scotland, Pleone said. We could take her now."

"Yes, yes, take her to Ellie. At once," Aunt May gasped. "Go upstairs and pack your things, all of you."

Troy and Harmony wasted no time. They dashed indoors and raced up the stairs in long strides. Aunt May, looking perfectly distracted, with her hair unrolling in long lumps, seized Hayley's hand and rushed her upstairs in a rattle of necklaces. When they reached Hayley's room, Aunt May dragged Hayley's little suitcase from under her bed, shook her head – causing more hair to unroll – and hunted in a cupboard until she found a big duffel bag. Into this she crammed all Hayley's new old clothes as fast as Hayley could pass them to her. She was just forcing Hayley's brush and comb in on top of Hayley's washing things, when Troy and Harmony arrived at a gallop, Troy with a huge backpack and Harmony carrying a bulging airline bag.

"Got everything?" Aunt May said.

"Not quite," Harmony said. "I had to leave my good dress. Can you hang—?"

She was interrupted by the crunching of wheels on the driveway outside.

"Oh, my God!" gasped Aunt May. "He's here already!"

She tore aside the blowing white curtains. They all looked down from Hayley's window at a taxi drawing up by the front door and at Mercer and Tollie going out to meet it, followed by Aunt Alice, Aunt Geta and Aunt Celia. Somehow they all managed to look like important people coming to meet a visiting president. Mercer actually bowed as the taxi door slammed open and Uncle Jolyon climbed out. Uncle Jolyon's blue eyes glared and, among his white beard, his mouth was almost a snarl. Hayley had never seen anyone look so thunderously angry. She backed away as Aunt May gently let the curtain fall back across the window.

"I'll go down and hold him up as long as I can," Aunt May said. "Do your best, Harmony." Necklaces clashing, hair flying, she ran out of the room.

Hayley listened to Aunt May's slippers thudding away down the stairs and wondered what they *could* do. At the very least, Uncle Jolyon was going to send her back to Grandma. But now she knew some of the things Uncle Jolyon had done and could do, she was quite sure she was going to be punished in a worse way than that.

"It's too late to get to the back door," Troy said. "He'll see us coming downstairs."

Chapter Ten

"I know what," Harmony said. "We need a science fiction strand. Find me one, Troy, quickly."

"The one I came back on just now," Troy said. "It was all futuristic stuff. Some of it's out on the upstairs landing."

Harmony said, "Right!" and seized Hayley's hand. Troy heaved up the duffel bag and they all three scurried out of the room and up the next flight of stairs. There at the top, almost exactly where the waterfall had started the night Hayley had arrived, stood a tall glass thing like a telephone box – or, even more, like a shower stall. Harmony pulled open its door and helped the other two to cram themselves and their luggage inside with her.

"A transportation booth?" Troy said. "Clever!"

"More than that," Harmony said, pressing away at a set of buttons beside the glass door. "It's a time booth too. I hope neither of you mind missing two days. We're going to catch the plane we were going to catch anyway and I hope we can do it before Uncle Jolyon realises. I'm hoping he doesn't know how good I am with the mythosphere and spends the next two days hunting for us. There!" Harmony said, pressing the large green button marked ENTER.

Without any feeling of change or movement, the view outside the glass door became the busy airport concourse that Hayley remembered from when she came to Ireland with Cousin Mercer. Troy slammed the door open and they ran. From then on it was all running, to the check-in, then up to Security and through the X-ray machine, on into the departure lounges and from there a race to the gates. As Harmony explained, waving their boarding passes as they pelted to where a loudspeaker was telling them that the flight to Edinburgh was now boarding, she had brought them here at the last minute to give Uncle Jolyon the smallest possible chance of finding them.

"And let's hope he's not waiting at the gate," she panted.

Hayley was terrified. Though she didn't at all understand why, it was clear to her that *she* was the one Uncle Jolyon wanted to catch. She was so frightened that she somehow put on comet speed and arrived at the desk in front of the gate long before the other two.

"They're coming! They're just coming!" she told the man behind the desk. Then she was forced to wait, hopping from one leg to the other and anxiously scanning the little rows of seats and the wine shop opposite, in case Uncle Jolyon came storming along to get her. She was not happy until Harmony and Troy arrived and they were all allowed to hurry through a gangway and on to the plane itself. Then she did not dare move from the doorway until she had looked along the length of the plane and made sure that

Uncle Jolyon was not sitting in one of the seats, waiting.

An embittered-looking stewardess hurried them along to the front, where there were two pairs of seats facing one another. Harmony and Troy sat together with their backs to the pilot's cabin. Hayley sat opposite them, next to the empty seat, beside the tiny window. While the plane thrummed and hummed and started slowly rumbling out towards the runway, Hayley kept looking at that empty seat, expecting any moment to see Uncle Jolyon sitting in it. While the pilot spoke to them – something about going north to avoid a thunderstorm over the Irish Sea – Hayley could hardly listen.

Then, to Hayley's terror, the plane stopped, waltzing in place somewhere out in the middle of the airport. The stewardess came and stood by their seats and told everyone how to use the oxygen and the life jackets. Oh, go, go, *go*! Hayley thought, clenching her hands so that her nails dug in. She craned backwards out of the tiny window, expecting any second to see a taxi with Uncle Jolyon in it racing after the plane. She was still craning when the plane started to move again, rushing along the widest strip of concrete. It took her quite by surprise when she found she was looking *down* at the concrete and down at trees and tiny fields, and realised they were in the air.

"So far so good," Harmony said, unbuckling her safety belt.

The stewardess came round and contemptuously gave them each a cup of orange juice and a bun.

"I wish I could have wine," Troy said, looking at the bottles on the stewardess's trolley.

"Don't provoke her," Harmony said. "She'll say we're all too young."

Troy bit into his bun, grumbling, "I'm a *thousand* times older than she is."

"Hush," Harmony said. "Are you all right, Hayley?"

"Scared," said Hayley. She did not feel like eating her bun. "Why is Uncle Jolyon so angry about me?"

"Because you were supposed to stay with our grandparents," Harmony said.

"For ever, I think," Troy said. "Can I have your bun if you don't want it?"

Hayley handed it to him. "Why?" she asked. "*Really* for ever?"

Harmony nodded, with her smooth pretty face screwed up in distaste. "A long time ago," she said, "thousands of years ago, in fact, around the time your parents decided to get married, Uncle Jolyon went to a seer called the Pythoness and asked what would happen if they did get married. He disapproved, you see, because your father was a mortal man—"

"Just as if *he* wasn't having love affairs with mortal women all the time!" Troy said, tearing the wrapper off the bun as if he were skinning it alive. "Old hypocrite! He has love affairs all over the place, mortals, immortals, you name them! He's my father, you know, and Harmony's, and the father of all the cousins – old *goat*!"

"Yes, well," said Harmony. "Let me tell her the story. The Pythoness said that if Merope – your mother – ever married a mortal man, their offspring would strip Jolyon of his power. Jolyon was horrified and went storming back to stop the wedding. But he was too late. Your parents had been married while he was away seeing the Pythoness and gone to Cyprus for their honeymoon. Jolyon couldn't get at them there—"

"Cyprus belongs to Aunt Venus," Troy put in, munching.

"So he had to wait until they came home to Greece," Harmony said. "And while he waited, he made plans. He knew that nine-tenths of his power came from the mythosphere, but he also knew that *our* power comes from the mythosphere too, and he knew that we were all going to be on Merope's side, all Merope's sisters and their children *and* our grandfather, Atlas. Between us, we have almost as much power as Jolyon does. So the first thing he did was to order all of us to leave the mythosphere and live the way we do now, as ordinary people, and we obeyed him, because we didn't understand what he was after—"

"Jupiter, bringer of joy!" Troy said bitterly. "We've been pinned down like this for more than two thousand years now. And all because he was afraid of a *baby*!" He crunched the bun paper up savagely.

"Well, he *was* head god in those days," Harmony said. She sighed. "Nowadays, his power is in money as much as in the mythosphere. Grandpa has to hold up the world economy for him and Jolyon makes sure we're all in debt to him."

"But what about *me*?" Hayley demanded.

"The moment your parents came home with you," Harmony said, "he took you and planted you on your grandparents, with orders that you were not to grow up and not to know anything about your family. Grandma always does what Jolyon says – it's part of her strict outlook. And at the same time, he shoved Merope and your father off into the mythosphere and told everyone they were being punished for disobedience."

"Though, in actual fact," Troy said, "he never did forbid them to marry – or not that *we* ever heard."

Hayley thought, in a stunned way, about all her time living under Grandma's strict discipline. It had seemed like years and years and years. And this was not surprising, since it *had* been years and years. And she had thought it was just life. "I met my dad in the mythosphere," she said. "Being punished. He looked so *tired*, Harmony. I wanted to rescue him, but he said only my mum could do that. He thinks she's in a women's strand, somewhere wild."

"Then I think we should do our best to find her," Harmony said. "We could hardly be in much more trouble now Tollie and Mercer have told Uncle Jolyon about the game. *Blast* Tollie!"

"That Autolycus," Troy said gloomily. "He really hates Hayley, doesn't he? He stole stuff from your father, Hayley, and your father caught him at it. I think that's why."

Harmony said, equally gloomily, "I don't think Tollie *needs* a reason to do the things he does. So if we look for Merope—"

"I have to have a star off Orion's bow too," Hayley said. "Flute said I had to give him one for stealing the apple."

Troy whistled. Harmony said, "Flute?" with her smooth forehead all wrinkled. Then the wrinkles cleared away and she said, "Oh, you mean one of those two who own the apples?"

Hayley nodded. "They're twins. They take turns at standing in the sun. I call them Flute and Fiddle, but who are they really, Harmony?"

Harmony looked at Troy, who shook his head, shrugged and said, "No idea."

"No more have I," Harmony confessed. "I've always called them Yin and Yang, because you have to call them *something*, and sometimes I wondered if they might be angels, but I really don't know. And I'll tell you this, Hayley. They always make you give them a fee for one of the apples, but I've never known them ask for anything as important as a star. The most *I've* had to give them is my old flute – or once they asked for the Old Soldier's violin – but otherwise it's just a blue bead or a farthing or a shoelace. Nothing really. If they've asked for one of Orion's stars, it must be serious. We'll look into that. But let's get back to Merope. What are the women's strands?"

"Witches," Troy suggested. "Suffragettes, Amazons, the Pythoness, Saint Ursula?"

"Or all those boring ladies who waited in towers for their prince to come," Harmony added. "Rapunzel – *you* know. Oh lord! There's hundreds! What about that girl who went about making prophecies that no one believed?"

"None of those are wild," Troy pointed out. "Go back to witches."

"There are *thousands* of those," Harmony said. "And what about Boadicea? Jezebel?"

They were still making suggestions to one another when the plane landed in Edinburgh.

It took ages to get off the plane and into the airport building. Hayley became nervous all over again. There seemed ample time for Uncle Jolyon to pounce on them while they shuffled along to collect their baggage, or while they stood for minute after minute watching the empty luggage carousel go round and round.

"I've just thought," Troy said, as Hayley's duffel bag pushed the flaps aside and toppled on to the metal surface. "Uncle Jolyon knows where we're going. What's to stop him marching in on Mother and simply waiting for us at home?"

"I'm hoping," Harmony said, as her bag, followed by Troy's backpack, flopped out on to the carousel as well, "that it'll take him more than these two days to realise that. He's quite slow-witted, you know. Grab those, Troy, and let's get going."

Hayley followed them out through the building, fatalistically expecting Uncle Jolyon to be waiting outside for them. But the only person there was Aunt Ellie. Hayley would have known who she was, even without the way the other two dropped their bags and flung their arms round her. Aunt Ellie looked like Aunt May gone respectable.

"Mother!" Harmony cried out, nestling her smooth dark head against Aunt Ellie's carefully curled grey one.

"Good to see you, Mum!" Troy said, wrapping his arms around her neat grey suit. "This is Hayley. Hayley, meet my mother, Electra."

Just like Aunt May, Aunt Ellie dived forward and hugged Hayley. "My dear," she said. She sounded very Scottish. "I'm *so* glad you're here! Come along, all of you. The car's away over there, and you wouldn't believe how much it costs to park in this place, so please hurry. Besides, your Aunt Aster's waiting in it."

Harmony and Troy both groaned.

"I know, I know," Aunt Ellie said, hurrying them across the road. "I had to bring Aster. Jolyon said I wasn't to let her out of my sight. She's gone and formed a most *unfortunate* attachment to a great rough Highlander – at *her* time of life, I *ask* you! Even if

Jolyon hadn't told me to keep them apart, I would have put my foot down about it. The whole town's talking. To think of *my sister* causing all this scandal – it keeps me awake at nights! The man *haunts* the place!"

"Who is he?" Troy asked, trying to hitch the duffel bag on his shoulder alongside his backpack.

"The Lorrd knows!" said his mother, more Scottish than ever. "I think him to be some gamekeeper from one of those shooting preserves in the North. He carries a gun. Eats with his knife! Jolyon thinks him unspeakable."

"Was Uncle Jolyon here?" Harmony asked anxiously. "When?"

"Two days ago," Aunt Ellie said. "He seemed to think young Hayley was with me." At this, Troy and Harmony exchanged pleased, relieved smiles. "Hayley, what have you done to put Jolyon in this terrible mood?"

"I think," Hayley said timidly, "I wasn't supposed to have gone to Ireland."

"Now that is unreasonable of Jolyon," Aunt Ellie said. "Why ever *not*, you poor child?"

They had by then arrived beside a neat grey car.

Aunt Ellie bent down and shouted through its window at the dim figure sitting in the back seat. "Aster! Hayley's here! Open this window and say hallo to her. *Asterope*! Do you hear me?"

The window went down to reveal a pale faced little lady with a fluffy mass of faded fair hair. She fixed washed-out blue eyes on Hayley and quavered, "Pleased to meet you, Hayley. Your hair is very untidy."

Hayley stared at her. It was quite impossible to believe that this faded-out little woman could cause great rough Highlanders to haunt her. It just did not seem likely. "How do you do, Aunt Aster?" she said politely.

"Oh, not so bad," Aunt Aster quavered. "I'm a poor traveller, you know, and Electra does drive so dangerously."

When Troy had slung the bags into the boot and climbed into the back seat beside Hayley, and Harmony had settled in the front, the car set off so sedately that Hayley knew Aunt Aster had been talking nonsense. Aunt Ellie must have been one of the world's most cautious drivers. But Aunt Aster continued to talk nonsense. While they drove through the city, she kept quavering, "There's a red light on the other road, Electra. You have to stop." And when at last they came out into the country, she quavered, "Not so fast, Electra! You're doing nearly thirty!" or "There's a car coming, Electra. It's going to hit us. Stop until it's gone by!" or "Electra, here's a *bus*!"

Aunt Ellie took no notice and drove slowly on – although once or twice Hayley distinctly heard her mutter, "Silly bizzom!" - while the countryside became more and more beautiful around them. First it was sloping green fields with blue hills above, and then it was real mountains. Hayley leant forward to look at a long narrow loch surrounded in pine trees, among great brown and purple mountains swathed in drifting cloud. Whereupon Aunt Aster quavered, "Sit back, poor child. You'll get hurt if we stop."

Troy whispered into Hayley's other ear, "Isn't she a *pain*?"

Hayley said, "This country's *lovely*!"

"I agree," said Troy, at the same time as Aunt Aster quavered, "Oh, no, town is so *much* nicer! I can't wait to get back to town. It's civilisation."

into the mythosphere and build it properly. It was one of the most beautiful cities *ever.* I was busy marking out all the foundations when Uncle Jolyon stuck us all down on Earth like this."

Hayley thought that the city might be even better now Troy had spent hundreds of years building models of it. She was just going to suggest this to him when Aunt Ellie called out, "Come along, both of you. Supper's ready. Wash your hands." And they had to get up and leave the entrancing heaps of houses, walls and gardens.

The dining room was at the back of the house, where there was a big, low window open on to Aunt Ellie's garden and the misty, purple mountains beyond. The sweet, moist scent of Scotland blew in through it, across large oval plates of mixed grill that Harmony was putting down in each place. Those smelled equally lovely, but in quite a different way.

All in all, it was one of the most marvellous meals Hayley had ever had. The chief marvel was the tall cake-stand in the middle of the table. It had four round shelves, each one covered with a lace doily, and on each doily there was a loaded plate. The top layer held thin bread and butter, which you ate with the mixed grill and then with honey if you wanted to. Then you worked your way down to shiny currant teacakes and butter, and after that to scones, which you had with jam and cream. Hayley ate cautiously, pacing herself, with one eye on the bottom layer, where there was a large chocolate cake iced in squashy, thick chocolate. After the scones, she was wondering if she would have room for that cake.

"No cake for me," Aunt Aster said in a fading voice. "It's far too rich, Ellie."

As she spoke, the open window went dark. Hayley looked round to see the middle section of what must have been a huge man standing outside it. All she could see at first was a vast faded kilt with a battered and grubby sporran dangling on it and, below that, a glimpse of sharp, hairy knees. Then the man put his huge hands on the windowsill and bent down to push his big, bearded face into the room. The gun he had slung on one shoulder clattered on the window and made everybody jump.

"*Wumman*!" he bawled. "Wumman, you said you'd be doon at the hoose! Are you no coming?"

His voice made the whole room rattle. Its effect on Aunt Aster was extraordinary. She jumped to her feet with a shriek, crying out, "Oh! Ryan! So sorry! They *will* try to keep me from you!" and rushed towards the window. She was no longer a faded, moaning aunt, but a lovely young woman with a cloudy mass of bright golden hair. She looked almost as beautiful as Aunt Alice. When she reached the window, the huge Highlander held out both arms and Aunt Aster jumped into them as nimbly as an athlete. The Highlander gave a huge laugh and strode away with her, carrying her like a baby.

It happened so quickly that everyone was stunned, Aunt Ellie most of all. It was several seconds before Aunt Ellie sprang to her feet. "*Stop* her!" she said. "Stop him! Jolyon's forbidden it!" When no one else moved, she began dithering about. "What shall we *do*?" she said. "I'd better go after her. Oh, where did I put my handbag? He'll be carrying her down the street! What *will* the neighbours say!"

Harmony, Troy and Hayley stood up uncertainly.

Aunt Ellie glared at them. "Don't just *stand* there!"

she said. "Come and help me fetch her *back*!" She raced out into the hallway, rummaged for a desperate second or so among the things on the hall stand, found the handbag with a yell of relief and, with the bag held on high, crashed out through the front door.

By the time the other three reached the top of the drive, Aunt Ellie was already in the street, waving her handbag and shouting. Ahead of her, striding along with Aunt Aster in his arms, the huge Highlander was already halfway through the town.

"*Stop*!" shrieked Aunt Ellie, rushing after them. "Put her *down*! Aster, I forbid you to do this! Jolyon won't allow it! Think of the *neighbours*!"

"If she wants the whole town to know, she's going the right way about it," Troy remarked.

"Yes, she's lost her head, but we'd better do something to help, I suppose," Harmony said.

They set off at a trot after Aunt Ellie.

Far ahead of them, the huge Highlander strode purposefully on, taking absolutely no notice of Aunt Ellie's screaming pursuit. About halfway along a row of small grey houses, he veered off at a right angle and marched towards the middle house in the row. When he reached its shiny front door, he put out a huge foot, kicked the door open and bore Aunt Aster away inside. The front door shut with a slam in Aunt Ellie's face as she came pounding up. Aunt Ellie jumped up and down in frustration. She kicked the door, but it remained shut. Then she seized the little polished knocker and clattered it violently.

"*Aster!*" she screamed. "Asterope, let me in at *once*!"

Hayley trotted after Troy and Harmony, trying not to giggle. They passed house after house, some with lace curtains twitching and others frankly full of staring faces. While she gulped back her giggles, Hayley wrestled with her memory. She was sure she had seen this huge, bearded man before. His face, as it had loomed through the window, was definitely familiar, beard and all. She tried thinking of him as a more normal human size – and he was even more familiar. She tried him in different clothes. A suit? No. A robe then? No. How about fur then? *Yes!* She had seen him when Flute first took her into the mythosphere. He was that hunter in a leopardskin with the mighty bow, who looked so like a film star. Now how, why was he important?

Hayley had got as far as this when they reached the little house. Aunt Ellie was now kneeling on the sidewalk, shouting through the letterbox. "Aster, this is your sister! Let me *in*! How could you do such a wicked thing? Think of your *family*, Aster! *Let me in*!"

"Er, Mum," Harmony said gently, "don't you have Aunt Aster's spare key?"

Aunt Ellie swivelled round on her knees to look up at her. "Of course I have. That's why I brought my handbag."

"Then couldn't you let yourself in?" Harmony suggested.

Aunt Ellie came out of her frenzy a little, enough to climb to her feet and open her handbag. "Yes, yes indeed," she said. "I can go in and drag her away, can't I?"

"If you think this Ryan will let you," Troy muttered.

Ryan! Hayley thought. That's it! "Not Ryan," she said. "His name's Orion."

Troy and Harmony stared at Hayley. Aunt Ellie

fumbled up a jingling bunch of keys and found the one that fitted Aunt Aster's door. "There!" she said turning it in the lock. "Now we shall see!" With her grey hair standing wildly out all over her head and almost seeming to give off electric sparks, Aunt Ellie barged the door open and dived inside the house. "Come along!" her voice came back to them.

Rather hesitantly, Troy, Harmony and Hayley followed her indoors, into a tiny dark hallway. Harmony said, "Then you need to find his bow, don't you? I wonder if it's—"

A door slammed further inside the house. Uproar broke out. They could hear Aunt Ellie shrieking, Aunt Aster yelling and huge, rumbling shouts from the Highlander.

"Do you think we can do any good in there?" Troy asked.

"We'd only add to the noise," Harmony said. "Let's go home. We left supper on the table and the front door wide open."

"Poor old Aster," said Troy. "Why hasn't she the right to be happy? Yes, let's go."

"But his bow—" Hayley began as she turned unwillingly to go outside again. And stopped.

The front door had swung almost shut after they came in. Propped behind it, beside the hinges, where anyone might leave an umbrella or a walking stick – or even a gun, Hayley supposed – was a six-foot-tall *thing.* All she could see of it in the dim light was that it was very slightly bent and most beautifully made, with elaborate decorations down the flatter side, leading into the silver wire of the handgrip in the middle. But the advantage of the dim light was that Hayley could see that the middle of each coiled decoration held a small twinkling light, making a whole row of tiny twinkles.

"Look!" she said.

"Quick!" said Troy. "Get one off."

He and Harmony held the tall longbow steady while Hayley picked and peeled at one of the lower twinkles. To her relief, it came free quite easily and rolled into her palm like a small loose diamond. Very carefully, she zipped it away into the smallest of her trouser pockets.

"Now let's get out," Harmony said, whispering even

though the shouting in the back part of the house was louder than ever.

One by one, they slid themselves round the edge of the front door and out into the street.

As Troy slid out after Hayley, a taxi thundered to a stop in the road beside them. Its rear door burst open and Uncle Jolyon climbed swiftly out, glaring with anger. His belly heaved, his white beard bristled sparks like Aunt Ellie's hair, and his eyes were blue pits you did not like to look into.

All three of them backed against the wall of the house, where Harmony somehow managed a faint smile. "Hallo, Jolyon," she said.

The blue eye-pits blazed at her. "I'll deal with you in a moment," Uncle Jolyon said. "*All* of you." His head bent sideways to listen to the yelling from inside the house. "Orion's in there now with her, isn't he?" he said, and to the taxi, "Wait." To Hayley's extreme relief, he marched straight past her into the house, ducking his head to get through the door, and the door slammed shut after him.

"Run!" said Harmony. "Run for your lives to the mythosphere!"

Chapter Eleven

They ran. Harmony took the lead at first, across the road and up along the other side, until she came to a steep alley between the houses that plainly led upwards to the mountains. Hayley was so terrified that, as soon as the alley led them among moist slabs of granite and tufts of heather, she put on comet speed and sprinted ahead, with Troy and Harmony pelting to catch up.

"Wait!" Harmony panted. "Look where you're *going*, Hayley!"

Hayley did not care where she was going. All she

wanted was somewhere to hide from Uncle Jolyon. She fled up a steep stony path and round several sharp bends until blessedly, blindingly, damp white fog began to blow around her. She slowed down a little so as not to lose the others. "Trees!" she said frantically, more or less to herself. "I want trees to hide in."

"He can blast trees," Troy panted.

"Trees – somewhere where Flute and Fiddle are," Hayley insisted, and ran on.

The fog, very thick now, and still blowing in gusts around her, began to grow darker, as if night was coming on. Well, I suppose we did just have supper, Hayley thought. She ran on upwards into increasingly blue-dark mist, where she thought she could just glimpse streaks and flickers of sunset up ahead.

In her terror, she almost didn't notice the trees when she did find some. What came to her first was their smell. Pine trees, she thought. A tarry, spicy smell. Thank goodness! Oddly enough, the streaks and flickers of red light were brighter now, and they had a smell too. Wood smoke.

Here Harmony stopped her by grabbing both her

shoulders. "Slow *down*, Hayley! I think we're on a really dangerous strand here. We have to be *careful*!"

Hayley found that they were standing on dry grass in a thick forest of pine trees. In the misty near-dark it was hard to see the pines except as great black cone shapes in all directions. Most of them had wide lower branches that swept right to the ground. But something was definitely burning up ahead and it gave enough light for Hayley to see just how dense and green and prickly those lower branches were.

Several long-legged dog shapes went trotting lightly and springily across the path ahead.

Wolves! Hayley thought. Unless they're something worse! She hardly dared move.

"See what I mean?" Harmony whispered.

"What's that noise?" said Troy.

It was screaming, but it was singing too – very bad, discordant singing, as if a large choir of ladies had each decided to sing a different song as loudly as they could. It seemed to be coming down the slope towards them. There were shrieks of joy and shrieks of something worse. "Eye-oh, eye-oh," sang the choirs.

"Oh dear," Harmony said. "I think these are the Maenads."

For some reason, Grandpa had never told Hayley anything about the Maenads, but she had no need to ask what they were. They arrived as Harmony spoke, under a blinding mass of crackling pine torches. They were a horde of mad women in tattered clothes, screaming, singing, imitating cats, dogs and eagle cries, dancing and galloping downhill. Their hair was loose and streaming. All of them were splashed with blood: some of them were covered in it. The wood smoke from the torches was suddenly overwhelmed by a smell like a butcher's shop where somebody had spilt a barrel of wine, and by the thick, sweaty smell of dirty women.

Harmony took hold of Hayley's arm and Troy's and dived with them under the trailing branches of the nearest pine tree. "Don't move, Troy," she whispered. "They kill men."

They did too. Hayley could not resist putting out one finger and pushing aside one prickly pine frond. The first thing she saw was a woman carrying a bearded man's head on a pole. Blood from the head was rolling down the pole, dripping on the woman's face and hands and plopping into her laughing mouth. "Look what *I've* got! Look what *I* did!" the woman yelled. She was crying as well as laughing. Tears were making white lines through the blood on her face.

Another woman came along with a huge earthenware jar of wine and tipped it into the first woman's face. "Drink up!" she shrieked. "Drown your sorrows!"

Someone behind those two screamed, "There's a man here! A *man*, everybody! I can smell him. He's under that tree!"

Next second, the entire screaming crowd was rushing down upon the pine tree where Troy, Harmony and Hayley were hiding. Torches fizzed against the pine needles. Wine showered through the overhanging boughs, and dozens of sticky, bloody hands reached through the branches to grab unerringly at Troy. He was seized by his hair and his shirt and his hands, even by his legs, and dragged out into the open.

"Pull him apart! Pull him to pieces!" all the women shouted.

Harmony plunged out after Troy and grabbed the back of his shirt. "No! Don't! Stop!" she shouted back. "You mustn't! He's the one who's going to build the great town of Troy!"

Hayley plunged out after her and tried to help pull Troy away, but by this time several women had hold of each of Troy's arms and were hauling on him like a tug-o-war. Troy screamed.

"Help!" Hayley yelled. "Oh, please, someone *help*!"

Somebody came up beside Hayley and said, "Is no good, not now they got him."

Hayley turned and saw fine white hair, lurid under the torchlight and spattered with blood. The hair surrounded an ugly pink face. "*Martya!*" Hayley said and threw her arms round Martya. "Oh, Martya, I'm so *glad* to see you!"

Martya's pale eyebrows went up. "Is most unusual," she said. "No one is glad me to see, ever."

"I am," Hayley said. "*Please* help us rescue Troy."

"But this is not why I come," Martya protested. "I am

here for telling you your mama is one of these soaked-in-wine women. She up here, up the hill. Come."

"But Troy—" Hayley said. She felt torn in two, almost as badly as Troy was being torn. She looked over at him to see that he was fighting back now, kicking women's shins and bucking about to get his arms free. But more and more shrieking women were piling in on him and on Harmony too. Other women laughingly held their torches high, lighting the struggle into wild, flickering shadows.

Martya watched the fight in a morose, critical way. She shrugged. "They got him," she said. "Only way would take their mind off him was be a person threw golden apples in their middles."

"Oh, why didn't you say so *before*?" Hayley gasped, frantically unzipping pockets. "I've got three – somewhere."

She finally found an apple by feel, feather light and plastic, and dragged it out. As she drew back her arm to throw it, it felt heavier somehow and gave out a strong smell of live apple, as strong as the smell of wine and blood and wood smoke. She hurled it as hard as she could into the mass of struggling women. It arced among the flames, shining pure strong gold, and thumped off someone's back.

The effect was instant. That woman, and at least six others, turned round at once and scrambled to grab it as it rolled downhill among everyone's feet. Much encouraged, Hayley found the second apple and hurled it, with a smack, into someone's face. This woman went down under the rush of the rest trying to catch it before it rolled under a tree. Hayley threw the third, simply into the remains of the fighting. It seemed even heavier and more golden than the first two. And it was as if all three apples had a will of their own. No matter how many hands grabbed for them, they bobbled out of reach, tumbling, dodging and rolling away, faster and faster, flashing in the torchlight. In seconds, every single woman had left Troy alone in order to chase the apples away downhill. He was left standing by the pine tree, with Harmony kneeling beside him.

"Thank goodness!" said Hayley. "Now show me my mum, Martya, quick."

"Can do," Martya said. She took Hayley's hand and pulled her uphill to another place among the pine trees, where another gaggle of crazy women were galloping round and round a huge wine jar. Nearly all of these women had dark hair, flying loose and sticky with wine and blood, but, as the howling crowd whirled past her for the second time, Hayley saw that one of them had fair hair. She was not easy to spot. Her hair was yellower than Martya's and mostly drenched in wine and – yes – quite a lot of blood too. Who cares? Hayley thought. She rushed up to that one and grasped her firmly by one flailing arm.

The woman staggered to a stop in front of her and put one hand up to her head. "Huh?" she said vaguely.

Hayley looked eagerly up into her face and – even in the uncertain light of the torches – she had no doubt. This was the woman in the wedding photograph. She was filthy and she was drunk and she looked rather older, but she was the same one. "Mother," she said. "Mum. I'm Hayley."

"Huh?" the woman said again.

"Patience I lose!" Martya said. "Patience I never have

much." She marched up to the woman and clapped her hands loudly in front of the vague face. "*Merope*!" she bawled. "Here your daughter is. Wake up and get pies out of eyes *now*!"

Merope blinked. Her face began slowly to wake up into the expressions of someone alive and attentive. "Did you say —?" she began.

Before she could say any more, the person in charge of the riot arrived, striding up to them in rather a hurry. He was a tall man dressed in animal skins, and he had a big hat on that seemed to be made of vine leaves. "Hey, girls!" he said merrily. "You three are forgetting to dance."

Martya just stared at him, looking uglier than usual. Hayley found she could not meet his eyes and looked down instead at his knee-high sandals and his big dirty toes sticking out of the front of them. Merope started to pull her arm away from Hayley in order to turn back into the dancing. Hayley hung on to her in a panic. She was not going to lose her mother as soon as she had found her.

"Did you know," she said to the man, in a high

panicky voice, "did you know that there's three golden apples from the star trees down there?"

He was very interested. "Really?" he said. "Where would those be?"

Hayley pointed, in probably quite the wrong direction. The man laughed gladly and set off that way, first in big strides and then almost running.

"Good done," Martya said as he disappeared in the darkness among the trees. "That is how to get rid of a god quick."

"What are you talking about?" Merope said. "What god?"

"Bacchus," Martya said. "Is god of booze. He got you tight."

"Never mind him," Hayley said. "Mother, I've found Dad, but he says only you can rescue him. He's in a place where they make him do unending work."

"What? My poor Sisyphus!" Merope said. "How long have I been here?"

"Centuries," said Martya. "This way, come. I have transport."

They set off downhill again. Hayley still hung on to

Merope's arm, but now it was less to keep her from rejoining the riot and more because she had a mother at last, which was a thing more wonderful than the mythosphere. With every step, Merope seemed to become more awake and more of a person. At first she smiled down at Hayley in a bewildered way. Then she said, "I can't believe this!" and wiped her hand down her tattered skirt. "I'm so filthy and sticky. I can hardly believe you're really Hayley – though I know you are. I remember you as a tiny baby. And," she said to Martya, "I don't understand about you at all."

"I help Hayley," Martya said. "I go adventuring to the Pleiades and they try to make me work. Hayley buys me lovely shoes. Look." She stopped and held one foot up. In the murky light Hayley could just see that Martya was wearing the pink shoes with cowboy fringes.

They went on, and the light grew better. Someone had stuck one of the flaring torches in the ground and, by its light, two tall people with white hair were anxiously examining Troy. "I'm all right," Troy was telling them. "None of this blood is mine. Honestly."

"Are you sure? Your face is pretty scratched,"

Harmony said. She was standing next to Troy, shivering. "I *hate* those Maenads!"

Hayley cried out with relief and dragged her mother over to them. There she risked letting go of Merope so that she could hug the two tall men. "Flute!" she said. "Fiddle! I *knew* you were around here somewhere!"

Flute patted Hayley's shoulder. "Did you get my star?" he asked.

While Hayley was nodding and saying to Flute, "It's in my smallest pocket," Fiddle spoke to Martya over Hayley's head. "Nice to see you again Yaga. Don't tell me you're doing good deeds now!"

"Only to Hayley," Martya said. "Her mother is this sticky Merope here."

"Oh, wonderful!" Harmony said. She took hold of both Merope's blood and wine covered hands. "I'm so glad to see you again, Aunt Merry."

"Hey, listen!" Troy said. "Look."

From downhill came a sound that was definitely from a car fighting its way up the mountain in low gear. The beams from its headlights swung this way and that among the trees as the car turned the corners of the steep track. They almost could have been searchlights hunting for someone.

"That's Uncle Jolyon's taxi," Hayley said.

Chapter Twelve

Everyone knew it was Uncle Jolyon. Troy and Harmony looked at one another, wondering what to do.

"Is no problem." Martya said. She clicked her fingers towards a dark clump of trees on the other side of the path. Part of the clump immediately rose up into a tall, square shape. It unfolded two long legs like chicken legs and stalked towards them. When it reached Martya, it stopped and let down a ladder from the balcony on its front. "Is my hut," Martya said. "Up, all! Up, up, up!"

Flute took hold of Hayley and pushed her up the

ladder. The rest followed, Fiddle pushing Merope, who kept getting her legs wrapped up in the rags of her dress, and Harmony helping Troy because Troy was still shaky. Martya came up last and the ladder came up with her. As soon as Martya was on the balcony, the hut turned and started walking away, creaking all over from the weight of seven people.

"You must show the way," Martya said to Fiddle.

Fiddle nodded and pointed more to the left. The hut turned again and went crashing and swishing across the mountainside. Before the trees quite closed in behind it, Hayley and Troy, craning anxiously from a corner of the balcony, saw the taxi arrive in the glade beside the flaring torch and go roaring on past, as if the driver had not realised that anyone had been there.

"Oh good!" said Hayley.

"He'll catch up in the end," Flute said to her. "Be ready with your star when he does. I'll tell you what to do."

The hut paced onwards. Fiddle kept pointing the way and the hut walked where his finger pointed. Hayley looked down at the toes of its big bird feet and then up to see that Fiddle was taking them across the mythosphere. The great feet goose-stepped from pine needles to rock, then into a desert, then on to a busy motorway, where they miraculously missed all the cars, and from there to a floaty pink strand. Here one of the great feet nearly went straight through the floatiness, but the hut saved itself with a twist and a twitch and strode on to a much firmer blue strand. Finally it marched into some kind of industrial estate full of cars parked beside low white buildings. The hut tramped straight across this place, kicking cars aside and crunching through the corners of buildings, until it came to a low white block labelled STONE BROS LTD in big red letters. Hayley somehow expected it to stop here, but instead it simply kept on and stamped on the building. Half the wall fell in and the hut came to a halt, marching in place and creaking and groaning all over, while glass tinkled and lumps of concrete and flat pieces of wall fell this way and that. When it had made a big hole in the building, the hut stopped trampling and let down its ladder.

"Come on," Flute said. "Quickly." He pushed Merope and Hayley on to the ladder. "The rest of you had better stay here," he said over his shoulder as he followed Hayley and Merope down.

Hayley seized her mother's hand and they ducked in together through the crumpled, sagging hole. Inside, the striplights were on and everyone was working away at their desks, just as if nothing had happened at all – except that the nearest people wearily slapped their hands down on their piles of paper as the wind from the broken wall threatened to blow them away and people further from the damage irritably blew and waved at the dust from the breakage. Hayley spotted her father at his desk in the far corner, working harder than anyone else there, and began dragging her mother towards him. But, halfway there, Merope saw him too, let go of Hayley's hand and rushed across between the desks. She knocked several trays of paper flying, but people simply sighed and bent to pick them up, without seeming to notice anything else.

"Cyrus!" Merope shouted. "My Sisyphus!"

It rang round the room and several people actually looked up. Hayley's father looked up among the rest. When he saw Merope bearing down on him, filthy hair flying, rags streaming, he stopped working, leant back and smiled. And smiled. Merope put both sticky hands down on his IN-tray and smiled back. They both smiled and gazed as if there was nothing else in the world.

"Oh, come on! Come *on*!" Hayley said to them, hopping from foot to foot.

She could see the woman who did not want to ladder her tights marching towards them from the other end of the room. The woman had been carrying a massive pile of folders, but she dumped those angrily on the nearest desk and strode swiftly down the aisle to the desk in the corner.

"We have to *go*!" Hayley said.

But her parents took not the slightest notice, until the woman came right up to them and shoved Hayley aside. "Leave here at once," she said to Merope. "You're interrupting this prisoner in his work."

Merope turned to look at her, slow and astonished. "I'm what?" she said.

"Distracting the prisoner. Trespassing," the woman said. "You've no business to be here. You must have escaped from another strand."

"That's right," Merope said. "And I've come to fetch my husband away from this one."

"You can't do that," the woman said.

Merope stood up to her full height, inches taller than the neat woman. Despite her torn and filthy dress, she was suddenly majestic. Her hair, clotted with blood and stained with wine, swirled outwards from her head and became bright gold, brighter even than the golden apples had been. Hayley stared, awed and admiring. My mother really is a sort of goddess! she thought.

"How *dare* you!" Merope said. "How *dare* you speak like that to a daughter of Atlas! No one here is a prisoner. They are all in unlawful captivity." Her voice rose, like a powerful singer's. "You're all free," she cried out. "Get up and leave, all of you."

The people at the desks looked up, astonished and unbelieving at first; but when Merope held out her hand to Hayley's father and he got up and came to her, still smiling, the rest began to stand up, hesitantly in ones and twos. As Merope held out her other hand to Hayley and began to sweep the pair of them across the room, everyone seemed to see that she meant what she said. They jumped up and made for the doors.

"Stop!" the neat woman called out. And when no one took any notice, she wailed, "How am I going to get all the forms filled in?"

"Try filling them in yourself," Merope said over her shoulder.

They reached the break in the wall and there was the ladder into the hut and Flute standing beside it. He was looking very impatient by then. He more or less hurled Hayley up the rungs and then hoisted Cyrus after her. Hayley's father had evidently become very stiff from sitting at the desk for so long. Merope seemed to float up and Flute scrambled after her.

"We've got him!" Hayley said joyfully to Fiddle as she reached the balcony.

"Good," Fiddle said. He looked at Martya. "Shall we go?"

"Instant," Martya agreed.

The hut tramped its feet and smartly goose-stepped itself into facing the other way.

And stopped.

Uncle Jolyon was standing in the way, with his taxi throbbing behind him. He seemed huge, and solid as a mountain. As everyone clutched the balcony rail and stared, he grew even vaster, until he was gazing down at them, with a sort of dishonest, implacable pity. His voice was as large as the rest of him.

"Shame," he thundered. "You all thought you were so clever, didn't you? But nobody ever really gets the better of *me*. And I'm very good at devising punishments for people who don't do what I want. You are all going to have a very nasty time, now and until the end of time. Trust me."

"I am not yours," Martya said. "There is nothing you can do to me."

"What makes you so sure of that?" Uncle Jolyon thundered back.

Hayley gazed up at his vast bulging shirt front in despair. Just as everything seemed to coming right! she thought. But as Martya said angrily, "Because I am the greatest witch that ever lives!" Hayley's attention was pulled that way. She saw Flute's big hand, down by Flute's side, making gestures to her to fetch out the star from Orion's bow. Hayley didn't dare nod. She dipped her chin at Flute and, furtively, gently, she put her hand to her smallest pocket and began unzipping it.

"What have you done to Orion?" Harmony asked suddenly and made Hayley's heart stutter, in case Uncle Jolyon noticed what she was doing.

"Orion?" Uncle Jolyon boomed. "I put him back amongst the stars of course – for keeps this time. Asterope's up there too, as far away from him as she can be."

"But why shouldn't they get together?" Troy said.

"Because they dipleased me," rumbled Uncle Joylon. "The man's a womaniser."

"So are you," Troy pointed out.

"Exactly. And I don't want any rivals," Uncle Jolyon boomed. "You, my boy, are now going to spend eternity being punished for your cheek. I haven't decided what to do to you yet, but I know you'll never, ever get to build your city."

While they talked, Hayley got her pocket unzipped and felt the star, tiny, warm and faintly fizzing, roll into the palm of her hand. Flute gently edged up on one side of her and Fiddle on the other. "When I say *Now*," Flute murmured, in the faintest of whispers, "push it into him as high up as you can reach."

Merope said loudly, "This is entirely unjust. *I* think we've all been punished enough."

"I don't," Uncle Jolyon retorted. "You, my good woman, are going back where you were, and so are you, Sisyphus, only this time it will *hurt*. As for that Hayley— Where *is* Hayley?"

Hayley was so much smaller than everyone else and Uncle Jolyon now so huge that he evidently had trouble picking her out from among the crowd on the balcony. Flute grinned at Fiddle and Fiddle nodded at Flute, and they both obligingly seized Hayley and boosted her upwards towards Uncle Jolyon's vast face. Hayley found herself travelling up what seemed half a mile of shirt front.

"*Now*!" said Flute.

Hayley put out her hand with the star in it and pressed it with all her strength into the middle of Uncle Jolyon's bulging chest. It twinkled there for just a second and then seemed to dissolve into his enormous body.

Uncle Jolyon made a strange noise, like a very deep

organ pipe, and began to spread. He spread and he spread, and grew fainter and more gaseous as he enlarged, and moved away backwards as he grew fainter. Stinging coldness came off him. After that he moved away so rapidly that Hayley could soon see that he had now become a globe, a vast, sulky, yellowish thing, that spread and backed away and spread as it receded, until it was a yellow disc, blotched and banded with dreary red. Then it was shining a circle, and finally it became a large bright star up in the sky.

"Ah," said Harmony. "The planet Jupiter."

"Yes," said Flute. "He can't do much harm to anyone as a planet."

"Or only the usual sidereal influences," Fiddle said. "And those are generally rather jolly."

They both grinned at Hayley as they lowered her back to the balcony.

"We go now," Martya announced. "I need my forest."

The hut at once jolted into its goose-step stride and took them away through the industrial estate – which now had a seedy, abandoned look – and then, in remarkably few strides, out on to a mountainside scattered with pine trees. After a few more strides, it stopped in a level place where they could look down on the respectable grey town where Aunt Ellie lived.

Everybody except Martya climbed down the ladder. Hayley was last because she stopped to hug Martya. Martya once again looked extremely surprised, as if nobody else had ever wanted to hug her.

"I'll come and visit you in the mythosphere," Hayley called as she too climbed down. She ran over and took hold of both her parents' hands. I can live with them now! she thought blissfully. No more Grandma. And, whenever I want to, I can go and be a comet.

"We shall be leaving now," Flute said to her. "This phase is over, so my brother and I change places again."

"I've always wondered when you did that," Harmony said. "Is it often?"

"Whenever we complete a new strand in the mythosphere," Fiddle told her. His sober dark suit, as he stood there, was slowly flushing green in the grey evening light. But his eyes still shone blue. Flute's baggy green clothes were fading to a severe grey, although they remained baggy and his white hair still blew about on his shoulders.

Hayley thought, I'll still be able to tell them apart in future. She watched the brothers smile at each other and then walk past one another, Fiddle striding to the left and Flute going to the right. A moment later, they were gone.

Everyone let the hut stride away too and began to walk, rather aimlessly, down the mountain.

"Where would you like the three of us to live?" Hayley's father said to Merope. "I fancy going back to Greece myself."

"Greece will have changed quite a lot since you were last there," Merope said. "I don't think you'll be a king there any more. Let's go to Cyprus again." She shivered in the quiet evening air. "It's just as warm as Greece there."

"Oh, but!" Hayley cried out. "If we live abroad, how can I see Troy and Harmony ?"

Troy laughed. "Don't worry. You'll always find me in the mythosphere. I shall be working on my city there and I'll need you to design the gardens. And you'll run into Harmony all the time. She goes everywhere."

"All the same," Harmony said, watching Merope shiver, "I think we should go home first. Mother will be fussing, and Merope needs a bath and some better clothes."

"Oh, yes," said Troy. "And we never even started on that chocolate cake." He began to run downhill, but stopped at the next bend in the path, pointing downwards and laughing. When Hayley nosily ran along to see what was amusing him so, she found she could see down into the main street of the town. Strolling down the middle of it was the enormous Highlander, with Aunt Aster clinging lovingly to his arm.

"See that?" Troy said. "This is what happens now you've pinned Uncle Jolyon to the sky. We can all do what we want to do. At last!"

More than a Story

Author's Note 3

Golden Apples 6

Mythosphere Match 8

The Solar System 10

Starry Night 12

The Western Zodiac 14

Know Yourself Game 16

If you like, you'll love... 18

Answers 20

Sneak preview 21

Author's Note

About the Characters

The aunts are **THE PLEIADES**, often known as The Seven Sisters, a star cluster in the general region of The Great Bear. It is possible to count seven of them only out of the corner of your eye. In Ancient Greece, The Pleiades seemed to mingle freely with both mortals and gods, and at least three of them had a love affair with Zeus (Jupiter), chief of the gods of both Greece and Ancient Rome. Uncle Jolyon is **JUPITER**.

The Pleiades are:

MAIA, whose son by Jupiter is **MERCURY** (Mercer), the messenger of the gods

ELECTRA, whose children by Jupiter are Harmonia (Harmony) and the man who built and founded the great city of Troy and became its first king

ALCYONE, known to astronomers as Beta Tauri, who seems to have been too lofty to have a love affair with anyone

TAYGETA, whose children by Jupiter became the Spartans

CELAENO, one of the fainter stars, whose children by Jupiter became many of the other peoples of Ancient Greece

ASTEROPE, very much fainter than her sister stars

MEROPE, who married **SISYPHUS**, a mortal king in Ancient Greece. Sisyphus was later punished by having to roll a stone eternally up a hill. As soon as he got near the top, the stone would roll back down to the bottom of the hill again.

The parents of the Pleiades are **PLEONE** (known to astronomers as "a shell star") and **ATLAS**. Atlas was the last of the race of Titans, gigantic beings whom Jupiter defeated when he first came to power as chief of the gods. Some of the Titans were once gods themselves until Jupiter destroyed them. Atlas was spared on condition that he held the world up on his shoulders (although some versions say it was the sky he carries).

In spite of his mighty task, Atlas seems to have had time to fall in love with the nymph Hespera, by whom he had five daughters, known together as the **HESPERIDES**. These ladies guarded the golden apples in the Western Isles.

AUTOLYCUS (Tollie) is the son of Mercury by a mortal woman. He grew up to be a thief, trickster, cattle rustler and general bad man. Some of the cattle he stole belonged to Sisyphus.

ORION was a mighty hunter in Ancient Greece, who chased women as often as he chased animals. He seems to have gone after both the Pleiades and the Hesperides, and ended up by being placed in the heavens as a constellation which, to this day, is one of the most notable in the winter skies.

As for **HAYLEY** (Halley's Comet), it seems to me that the child of a star and a mortal king would almost certainly be a comet.

Golden Apples

Some of the many stories and myths containing golden apples.

Mythosphere Match

Can you match each person on the left with the correct object on the right?

Aladdin

Frodo Baggins

Sinbad

Alice

Baba Yaga

Medusa

Cinderella

Thor

King Arthur

Persephone

Bottle labelled "drink me"

Hammer

Excalibur

Pomegranate

Ring

Roc's egg

Glass slipper

Hut with chicken legs

Magic lamp

Snake hair

Answers on page 20.

The Solar System

The planets rotate around the sun on a fixed path or orbit. This diagram is like the picture Grandpa showed Hayley on his computer screen.

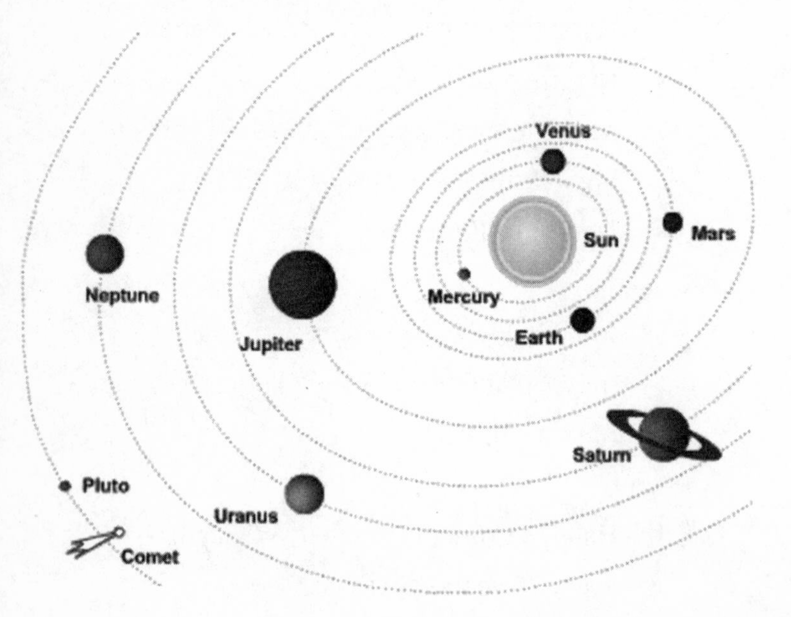

Jupiter is the largest planet in the solar system. It is bigger than all the other planets together.

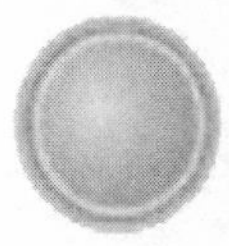

People used to make up silly sentences (known as mnemonics) using the initial letters of each planet to remember their order from the sun. The most well-known is: Mother Very Easily Made Jam Sandwiches Under No Protest.

In 2006 Pluto was reclassified as a minor planet. Unlike the planets, it has an elliptical orbit.

Halley's Comet is visible from Earth every 76 years. It was last seen in 1986 and will return in 2062.

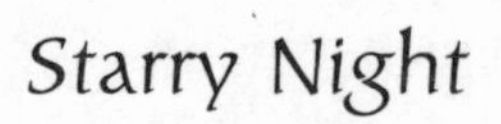

Starry Night

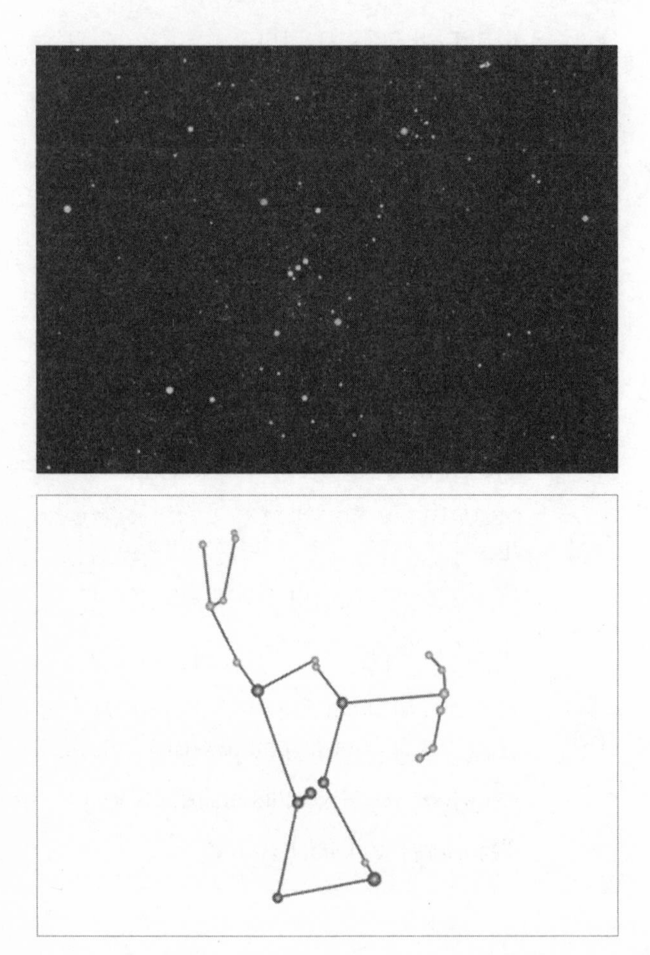

Orion is the brightest constellation in the winter sky.

The three stars across his "belt" are the easiest way to spot this group.

The stars are not really linked in any way, but ancient civilisations imagined the shape.

There are many myths about Orion the Hunter. One story says that he perpetually chases the Pleiades across the sky, while Taurus the Bull prevents him from ever reaching them.

You can find the "horns" of Taurus above and to the right of Orion. The cloudy cluster behind Taurus is the Pleiades.

The Western Zodiac

These are the sun signs. Which one were you born under?

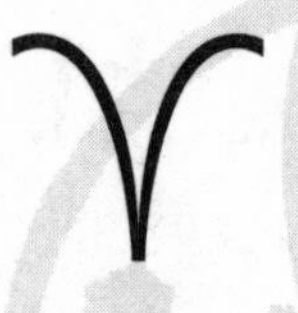

ARIES
The Ram
March 21st – April 20th

TAURUS
The Bull
April 21st – May 21st

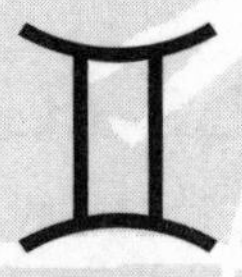

GEMINI
The Twins
May 22nd – June 22nd

CANCER
The Crab
June 23rd – July 23rd

LEO
The Lion
July 24th – August 23rd

VIRGO
The Ram
August 24th – Sept 23rd

LIBRA
The Scales
Sept 24th– Oct 23rd

SCORPIO
The Scorpion
Oct 24th – Nov 22nd

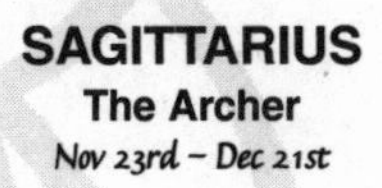

SAGITTARIUS
The Archer
Nov 23rd – Dec 21st

CAPRICORN
The Sea-goat
Dec 22nd– Jan 20th

AQUARIUS
The Water Carrier
Jan 21st – Feb 19th

PISCES
The Fishes
Feb 20th – March 20th

Know Yourself Game

The sun sign you are born under is supposed to give you certain personality traits. From the descriptions listed here, can you recognise yourself?

Hard worker, high standards, wise, fatalistic

Curious, open-minded, inventive, fickle

Kind, intuitive, protective, overbearing

Honest, enthusiastic, inspiring, fears responsibility

Creative, compassionate, romantic, unrealistic

Faithful, smart, persevering, stubborn

Earnest, sincere, a good friend, indecisive

Inventive, a good communicator, thoughtful, self-absorbed

Lively, friendly, generous, arrogant

A natural leader, patient, persistent, selfish

11. Passionate, vigorous, inquisitive, moody

Humane, charming, witty, critical

Answers on page 20.

If you like, you'll love...

If you liked reading The Game, you'll enjoy these other books by Diana Wynne Jones.

If you like **myths**, you'll love *Eight Days of Luke.*

When Luke turns up claiming that David has released him from prison, David doesn't know what to believe. But whenever he lights a flame, his new friend appears...

If you like **games**, you'll love *The Homeward Bounders.*

When Jamie discovers the sinister, dark-cloaked Them playing with human lives, he becomes part of their game. If he can get Home, he is free...

If you like **stars**, you'll love *Dogsbody.*

Sirius the Dog Star is sent to Earth as punishment. Here he is to live as a dog, unless he can discover a valuable device that has been lost.

If you like **crazy families**, you'll love *Archer's Goon*.

The trouble begins when the Goon moves into the kitchen and refuses to leave. It is then that the Sykes family discover that the town is being run by seven megalomaniac wizards!

If you like **time travel**, you'll love *A Tale of Time City*.

Vivian is kidnapped and taken to Time City, a place that exists outside time and space. But the city is crumbling, and unless Vivian can help discover the cause, all of history will end...

If you like **fairy tales**, you'll love *Howl's Moving Castle*.

When Sophie falls under a curse, she seeks help from the fearsome Wizard Howl, whose appetite, they say, is satisfied only by the hearts of young girls...

Answers

Mythosphere Match

Aladdin + Magic lamp

Sinbad + Roc's egg

Baba Yaga + Hut with chicken legs

Cinderella + Glass slipper

Thor + Hammer

Frodo Baggins + Ring

Alice + Bottle labelled "drink me"

Medusa + Snake hair

King Arthur + Sword in the stone

Persephone + pomegranate

Know yourself Game

Is your personality written in the stars? Or is it all just a load of moonshine?

1. Capricorn
2. Gemini
3. Cancer
4. Sagittarius
5. Pisces
6. Taurus
7. Libra
8. Aquarius
9. Leo
10. Aries
11. Scorpio
12. Virgo

If you were wrong, go back and check which one is supposed to match you. Do you agree with it? Try the quiz on your friends and see how they match up.

A chaotically magical sequel to Howl's Moving Castle

HOUSE OF MANY WAYS

IN WHICH CHARMAIN IS VOLUNTEERED TO LOOK AFTER A WIZARD'S HOUSE

Sneak preview...

Mrs Baker had *forgotten* to pack the books. "Well," Charmain said, after an interval of blinking and swallowing, "I suppose I've never really been away from home before. Next time I go anywhere, I'll pack the bag *myself* and fill it with books. I shall make the best of it for now."

Making the best of it, she heaved the other bag on to the crowded table and shoved to make room for it. This shunted four milk jugs and a teapot off on to the floor. "And I *don't care*!" Charmain said as they fell. Somewhat to her relief, the milk jugs were empty and simply bounced, and the teapot did not break either. It just lay on its side leaking tea on to the floor. "That's probably the good side to magic," Charmain said, glumly digging out the topmost meat pasty. She flung her skirts into a bundle between her knees, put her elbows on the table, and took a huge, comforting, savory bite from the pasty.

Something cold and quivery touched the bare part of her right leg.

Charmain froze, not daring even to chew. This kitchen is full of big magical slugs! she thought.

The cold thing touched another part of her leg. With the touch came a very small whispery whine.

Very slowly, Charmain pulled aside skirt and tablecloth and looked down. Under the table sat an extremely small and ragged white dog, gazing up at her piteously and shaking all over. When it saw Charmain looking down at it, it cocked uneven, frayed-looking white ears and flailed at the floor with its short, wispy tail. Then it whispered out a whine again.

"Who are *you*?" Charmain said. "Nobody told me about a dog."

Great Uncle William's voice spoke out of the air once more. "This is Waif. Be very kind to him. He came to me as a stray and he seems to be frightened of everything."

*